"Tongues are wagging. It is Rescue River."

"Gossip central," he agreed.

"And speaking of wagging tongues," she said, "imagine what people will assume if you come and live in the guesthouse. They'll think we're a couple. I'm not comfortable with that."

"I understand." He looked down at his hands, traced a scar that peeked out from his shirt cuff. "I'm not exactly a blue-ribbon bronco."

"Vito!" She sounded exasperated. "You haven't changed a bit since you had to try on six different shirts for the homecoming dance."

"That was a long time ago. And the truth is, I have changed."

She rolled her eyes. "You're still good-looking, okay? Women don't mind scars." Then she pressed her lips together as her cheeks grew pink.

His heart rate accelerated just a little. Why was she blushing? Did she think he was good-looking?

But of course, she hadn't seen the worst of his scars.

And even if there was a l[...] them, it couldn't go anyw[...] living with a secret he co[...]

Lee Tobin McClain read *Gone with the Wind* in the third grade and has been a hopeless romantic ever since. When she's not writing angst-filled love stories with happy endings, she's getting inspiration from her church singles group, her gymnastics-obsessed teenage daughter and her rescue dog and cat. In her day job, Lee gets to encourage aspiring romance writers in Seton Hill University's low-residency MFA program. Visit her at leetobinmcclain.com.

Books by Lee Tobin McClain

Love Inspired

Rescue River

Engaged to the Single Mom
His Secret Child
Small-Town Nanny
The Soldier and the Single Mom
The Soldier's Secret Child

Lone Star Cowboy League: Boys Ranch

The Nanny's Texas Christmas

The Soldier's Secret Child

Lee Tobin McClain

HARLEQUIN® LOVE INSPIRED®

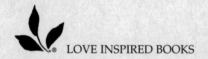

LOVE INSPIRED BOOKS

ISBN-13: 978-0-373-21432-7

The Soldier's Secret Child

Copyright © 2017 by Lee Tobin McClain

www.Harlequin.com

Printed in U.S.A.

I will give you a new heart and put a new spirit in you; I will remove from you your heart of stone and give you a heart of flesh.

—*Ezekiel* 36:26

To my daughter, Grace, who shows me
every day that families aren't about bloodlines;
they're about heart.

Chapter One

Lacey McPherson leaned back, propped her hands on the low white picket fence and surveyed the wedding reception before her with satisfaction. She'd pulled it off.

She'd given her beloved brother and his bride a wedding reception to remember, not letting her own antiromance attitude show. But she had to admit she'd be glad when her half-remodeled guesthouse stopped being a nest for lovebirds.

"Nothing like a spring wedding, eh, Lacey?"

She jumped, startled at the sound of the gruff, familiar voice right behind her. She spun around. "Vito D'Angelo, you scared me!" And then her eyes widened and she gasped. "What happened?"

His warm brown eyes took her back to her teen years. She'd been such a dreamer then, not good at navigating high school drama, and her brother's friend had stepped in more than once to defend her from girls who wanted to gossip or boys who tried to take advantage. She and her brother had welcomed invitations to the D'Angelo family's big, loud Italian dinners.

But now the most noticeable thing about his face wasn't his eyes, but the double scar that ran from his forehead to his jawline. A smaller scar slashed from his lower lip to his chin.

Instinctively she reached out toward his face.

He caught her hand, held it. "I know. I look bad. But you should see the other guy."

His attempt at a joke made her hurt more than it made her laugh. "You don't look bad. It's just…wow, they barely missed your eye."

Awkwardly, she tried to hug him with the fence in between.

He broke away and came inside through the open gate. "How're you doing, Lace? At least *you're* still gorgeous, huh? But you're too thin."

"You sound just like your grandma. And you're late for the wedding." Her heart was still racing from the surprise, both of seeing him and of how he looked.

She wanted to find out what had happened. But this wasn't the time or the place.

"Buck won't mind my being late. He looks busy." Vito looked past the wedding guests toward Lacey's brother, laughing and talking in the summer sun, his arm slung around his new bride. "Looks happy, too. Glad he found someone."

A slightly wistful quality in Vito's words made Lacey study her old friend. She hadn't seen him in almost ten years, not since he'd brought his army buddy home on a furlough and Lacey had fallen hard for the handsome stranger who'd quickly become her husband.

Back then, after one very stormy conversation, Vito had faded into the background. He'd been in the firestorm that had killed Gerry, had tried to save him and had written to Lacey after Gerry's death. But he'd continued on with another Iraq tour and then another. She'd heard he'd been injured, had undergone a lot of surgery and rehab.

Looking at him now, she saw that he'd filled out from slim to brawny, and his hair curled over his ears, odd for a career military man. "How long are you home?"

"For good. I'm out of the army."

"Out?" She stared. "Why? That was all you ever wanted to do!" She paused. "Just like Gerry."

"I felt awful I didn't make his funeral." He put an arm around her shoulders and tugged her to his side. "Aw, Lace, I'm sorry about all of it."

Her throat tightened and she nodded. Gerry had been dead for a year and a half, but the loss still ached.

A shout went up from the crowd and something came hurtling toward her. Instinctively she put her hands up, but Vito stepped in front of her, catching the missile.

Immediately, he turned and handed it to her.

A bouquet of flowers? Why would someone…

Oh. *The* bouquet. Gina's.

She looked across the crowd at her friend, glowing in her pearl-colored gown. Gina kept encouraging Lacey to date again. Happily in love, she wanted everyone to share in the same kind of joy.

The crowd's noise had quieted, and some of the guests frowned and murmured. Probably because Gina had obviously targeted Lacey, who'd been widowed less than two years ago. One of the older guests shook her head. "Completely inappropriate," she said, loud enough for most of those nearby to hear.

Well, that wouldn't do. Gina was a Californian, relatively new to Ohio and still finding her way through the unspoken rules and rituals of the Midwest. She hadn't meant to do anything wrong.

Lacey forced a laugh and shook the bouquet threateningly at Gina. "You're not going to get away with this, you know," she said, keeping her tone light. "I'm passing it on to…" She looked around. "To my friend Daisy."

"Too late." Daisy waved a finger in front of her face and backed away. "You caught it."

"Actually, Vito caught it," old Gramps Camden said. "Not sure what happens when a man catches the bouquet."

As the crowd went back to general talk, Lacey tried to hand off the bouquet to all the females near her, but they all laughingly refused.

Curious about Vito's reaction, she turned to joke with him, but he was gone.

Later, after Gina and Buck had run out to Buck's shaving-cream-decorated truck, heads down against a hail of birdseed, Lacey gave cleanup instructions to the two high school girls who were helping her with the reception. Then, after making sure that the remaining guests were well fed and happy, she went into the guesthouse. She needed to check on Nonna D'Angelo.

Having Nonna stay here was working out great. The light nursing care she needed was right up Lacey's alley, and she enjoyed the older woman's company. And the extra bit of income Nonna insisted on paying had enabled Lacey to quit her job at the regional hospital. Now that the wedding was over, she could dive into the final stages of readying the guesthouse for its fall opening.

Nonna D'Angelo had mingled during the early part of the reception, but she'd gone inside to rest more than an hour ago. Now Lacey heard the older woman crying and hastened her step, but then a reassuring male voice rumbled and the crying stopped.

Vito.

Of course, he'd come in to see his grandma

first thing. He hadn't been home in over a year, and they'd always been close.

She'd just take a quick peek to make sure Nonna wasn't getting overexcited, and then leave them to their reunion.

Slowly, she strolled down the hall to the room she'd made up for Nonna D, keeping her ears open, giving them time. She surveyed the glossy wood floors with satisfaction. The place was coming along. She'd redo this wallpaper sometime, but the faded roses weren't half-bad for now. Gave the place its historical character.

She ran her hand along the long, thin table she'd just bought for the entryway, straightened her favorite, goofy ceramic rooster and a vase of flowers. Mr. Whiskers jumped up onto the table, and Lacey stopped to rub his face and ears, evoking a purr. "Where's the Missus, huh?" she cooed quietly. "Is she hiding?"

Hearing another weepy sniffle from Nonna D, Lacey quickened her step and stopped in the doorway of Nonna's room.

"My beautiful boy," Nonna was saying with a catch in her voice. "You were always the good-looking one."

Vito sat on the edge of the bed, looking distinctly uncomfortable as Nonna sat up in bed to inspect his cheek and brush his hair back behind his ears.

She felt a quick defensiveness on Vito's behalf. Sure, the scars were noticeable. But to Lacey, they added to his rugged appeal.

Nonna saw her and her weathered face broke into a smile, her eyes sparkling behind large glasses. "There's my sweet girl. Come in and see my boy Vito."

"We talked already, Nonna." Vito was rubbing the back of his neck. "Lacey, I didn't realize you were taking care of my grandma to this extent. I'll take her home tomorrow."

"Oh, no!" Lacey said. "I'm so happy to do it!"

"I can't go home!" Nonna said at the same time.

"Why not?" Vito looked from Nonna to Lacey and back again.

"I need my nursing help," Nonna explained. "Lacey, here, is a wonderful nurse. She's practically saved my life!"

Lacey's cheeks burned. "I'm really a Certified Nursing Assistant, not a nurse," she explained. "And I haven't done anything special, just helped with medications and such." In truth, she knew she'd helped Nonna D'Angelo with the mental side as well as the physical, calming her anxiety and making sure she ate well, arranging some outings and visits so the woman didn't sink into the depression so common among people with her health issues.

"Medications? What's wrong?"

"It's my heart," Nonna started to explain.

Vito had the nerve to chuckle. "Oh, now, Nonna. You've been talking about your heart for twenty years, and you never needed a nurse before."

"Things are different now." The older woman's chin quivered.

He reached out and patted her arm. "You'll be fine."

Lacey drew in a breath. Should she intervene? Families were sometimes in denial about the seriousness of a beloved relative's health problems, and patients sometimes shielded their families from the truth.

"If you want to move your grandma, that's fine," she said, "but I'd recommend waiting a couple more weeks."

"That's right." Nonna looked relieved. "Lacey needs the money and I need the help."

Vito frowned. "Can we afford this?" He looked down at his grandma and seemed to realize that the woman was getting distressed. "Tell you what, Grandma, Lacey and I will talk about this and figure some things out. I won't leave without saying goodbye."

"All right, dear." She shot a concerned glance at Lacey.

She leaned down in the guise of straightening a pillow for Nonna. "I'll explain everything," she reassured her.

She led the way to the front room, out of earshot from Nonna D'Angelo. Then she turned to Vito, frowning. "You don't think I'm taking advantage of your grandma, do you?"

"No!" He reached for her, but when she took a step back, he crossed his arms instead. "I would never think that, Lacey. I know you. I just don't know if you've thought this through."

She restrained an eye roll. "You always did like to interfere when your help wasn't needed."

"Look, if this is about that talk we had years back..." He waved a dismissive hand. "Let's just forget that."

She knew exactly what he meant. As soon as Vito had found out Gerry had proposed, he'd come storming over to her house and pulled her out onto the front porch to try and talk her out of it. "You were wrong," she said now.

"I wasn't wrong." When she opened her mouth to protest, he held up a hand. "But I was wrong to interfere."

That wasn't exactly what she'd said, but whatever.

"But back to my grandma. I don't know what her insurance is like, but I know it hardly ever covers in-home nursing care. I'm living on limited means and until I get back on my feet—"

"It's handled. It's fine."

He ran a hand through his thick, dark hair. "She's always tended to be a hypochondriac—"

"A heart attack is nothing to take lightly."

"A *heart attack*?" Vito's jaw dropped. "Nonna had a heart attack?"

His surprise was so genuine that her annoyance about what she'd thought was neglect faded away. "About two weeks ago. She didn't tell you?"

"No, she didn't tell me. Do you think I'd have stayed away if I'd known?" His square jaw tightened. "Not a word. How bad was it?"

Lacey spread her hands. "Look, I'm just a CNA. You should definitely talk to her doctor."

"But from what you've seen, give me a guess."

Outside, she could hear people talking quietly. Dishes rattled in the kitchen, the girls cleaning up. She blew out a breath. "It was moderate severity. She had some damage, and there are some restrictions on what she can do. Changes she needs to make."

"What kind of changes?" He thrust his hands in his pockets and paced. "I can't believe she had a heart attack and I didn't know. Why didn't you call me?"

"It's her business what she tells people."

His mouth twisted to one side. "C'mon, Lace."

"I'm serious. Patients have the right to confidentiality. I couldn't breach that. In fact," she said, stricken, "I probably shouldn't have told you even now."

"You're my friend. You can tell me as a

friend. Now, what kind of changes? What does she need to do to get back on her feet?"

She perched on the arm of an overstuffed chair. "You can probably guess. It's a lot about diet. She needs to start a gentle exercise program. I have her walking around the block twice a day."

He stared. "Nonna's walking? Like, for exercise?"

"I know, right?" She smiled a little. "It wasn't easy to talk her into it. I make sure we have an interesting destination."

"How did you get so involved?"

She let her forehead sink down into her hand for just a second, then looked back up. Vito. He'd never take her seriously. He'd always been a big brother to her, and he always would be.

He held up a hand. "I'm not questioning it, Lacey. I'm grateful. And I feel awful having been out of the loop, not helping her. I've had lots of personal stuff going on, but that's no excuse."

His words flicked on a switch of interest

in her, but she ignored it. "I worked her hall at the hospital, and since she knew me, we talked. She was worried about coming home alone, but she didn't want to bother you, and your brother's far away. I was looking to make a change, anyway, moving toward freelance home care so I could have time to finish renovating this place." She waved an arm toward the unfinished breakfast area, currently walled off with sheets of plastic.

"So you made a deal with her." He still sounded a little skeptical.

"Yes, if that's what you want to call it." She stood, full of restless energy, and paced over to the fireplace, rearranging the collection of colored glass bottles on the mantel. "She's had a lot of anxiety, which is common in people recovering from a heart attack. She's on several new medications, and one of them causes fatigue and dizziness. The social worker was going to insist on having her go to a nursing home for proper care, which she couldn't afford, so this was a good arrangement." She looked over at him, mentally daring him to question her.

He rubbed a hand over the back of his neck. "A nursing home. Wow."

"It wouldn't have suited her."

"For how long? How long do you think she'll need the extra care?"

Lacey shrugged, moved an amber bottle to better catch the sun. "I don't know. Usually people take a couple of months to get back up to speed. And your brother's happy to pay for as long as we need."

Vito's dark eyebrows shot up. "She told him and not me?"

"She said you'd find out soon enough, when you came back home."

"And he's paying for everything?"

"He felt bad, being so far away, and apparently he begged her to let him help. Look, if you want to make a change in her care, I totally understand." It would mess up her own plans, of course; she'd given notice at the hospital only when she had this job to see her through, so if Nonna left, she'd have to apply for a part-time job right away. But Nonna was improving daily. If she had Vito with her, and he could focus on her needs, she'd probably be fine. A lot of her anxiety and depression stemmed from loneliness and fear.

Truth was, Lacey had found the older woman a hedge against her own loneliness, as her brother had gotten more and more involved in his wedding plans.

Now Buck and Gina and their dogs would be living in a little cottage on the other side of town. She'd see them a lot, but it wouldn't be the same as having Buck living here. "Whatever you decide," she said. "For now, we'd better go reassure your grandma, and then I need to attend to the rest of my guests."

Vito followed Lacey back into his grandmother's room, his mind reeling. Nonna had mostly raised him and his brother, Eugene, after their parents' accident, and she was one of the few family members he had left.

More to the point, he was one of *her* only family members, and he should have been here for her.

Everyone treated him like he was made of glass, but the fact was, he was perfectly healthy on the inside. His surgeries had been a success, and his hearing loss was corrected with state-of-the-art hearing aids, courtesy of the VA.

He just *looked* bad.

And while the scars that slashed across his face, the worse ones on his chest, made it even more unlikely that he'd achieve his dream of marriage and a large family, he couldn't blame his bachelorhood entirely on the war. Women had always liked him, yes—as a friend. And nothing but a friend. He lacked the cool charisma that most women seemed to want in a boyfriend or husband.

Entering his grandmother's room, he pulled up a chair for Lacey, and then sat down on the edge of Nonna's bed, carefully, trying not to jolt her out of her light doze. He was newly conscious that she was pale, and thinner than she'd been. A glance around the attractive bedroom revealed a stash of pill bottles he hadn't noticed before.

Nonna's eyes fluttered open and she reached out.

He caught her hand in his. "Hey, how're you feeling?"

She pursed her lips and glared at Lacey. "You told him about my heart."

"Yes, I told him! Of course I told him!" Lacey's voice had a fond but scolding tone. "You should have let him know yourself, Nonna. I thought you had."

He squeezed his grandmother's hand. "Don't you know I would've dropped everything and come?"

Nonna made a disgusted noise. "That's exactly why I didn't tell you. You and your brother have your own lives to lead. And I was able to find a very good arrangement on my own." She smiled at Lacey.

"It *is* a good arrangement, and I'm glad for it." Vito glanced over at Lacey, who had gotten up to pour water into a small vase of flowers.

With its blue-patterned wallpaper, lamp-lit bedside table and a handmade quilt on the bed, the room was cozy. Through the door of the small private bathroom, he glimpsed handicapped-accessible rails and a shower seat.

Yes, this was a good situation for her. "Look, I want to take you back to the house, but we'll wait until you're a little better."

Nonna started to say something, and then broke off, picking restlessly at the blanket.

"I haven't even been over to see the place yet," he continued, making plans as he thought it through. "I just got into town. But I'll check it out, make sure you've got everything you need."

"About that, dear…" Nonna's voice sounded uncharacteristically subdued.

"I hope you don't mind, but I'm planning to live there with you for a while." He smiled. It was true comfort, knowing he could come back to Rescue River anytime and find a welcome, a place to stay and a home-cooked meal.

Lacey nodded approvingly, and for some reason it warmed Vito to see it.

"Neither one of us will be able to live there," Nonna said, her voice small.

Lacey's eyebrows rose in surprise, and he could feel the same expression on his own face. "What do you mean?"

"Now, don't be angry, either of you," she said, grasping his hand, "but I rented out the house."

"You *what?*"

"When did you do that?" Lacey sounded bewildered.

"We signed the papers yesterday when you were out grocery shopping," Nonna said, looking everywhere but at Vito and Lacey.

"Who'd you rent it to?" If it had just been finalized yesterday, surely everything could be revoked once the situation was explained. Lacey hadn't said anything about cognitive problems, but Nonna *was* in her early eighties. Maybe she wasn't thinking clearly.

Nonna smiled and clasped her hands together. "The most lovely migrant family," she said. "Three children and another on the way, and they're hoping to find a way to settle here. I gave them a good price, and they're going to keep the place up and do some repairs for me."

"Nonna…" Vito didn't know where to begin. He knew that this was the way things worked in his hometown—a lot of bartering, a lot of helping out those in need. "You aren't planning to stay here at the guesthouse indefinitely, right? How long of a lease did you sign?"

"Just a year." She folded her hands on top of her blanket and smiled.

"A year?" Not wanting to yell at his aged grandma, Vito stood and ran his hands through his hair. "Either you're going to have to revoke it, or I'm going to have to find another place for you and me to live." Never mind how he'd afford the rent. Or the fact that he'd named Nonna's house as his

permanent residence in all the social services paperwork.

"No, dear. I have it all figured out." She
took Lacey's hand in hers, and then reached
toward him with her other hand. Once she
had ahold of each of them, she smiled from
one to the other. "Vito, if Lacey agrees, you
can stay here."

No. She wasn't thinking clearly. "Nonna,
that's not going to work. Lacey made this
arrangement with you, not with me." And
certainly not with the other guest he had in
tow. No way could Lacey find out the truth
about Charlie.

"But Lacey was thinking of getting another boarder for this period while she's remodeling. It's hard to find the right one,
because of all the noise." Lacey started to
speak, but Nonna held up a hand. "The noise
doesn't bother me. I can just turn down my
hearing aid."

Vito knew what was coming and he felt
his face heat. "Nonna…"

"Vito's perfect," she said, looking at Lacey, "because he can do the same thing."

Lacey's eyebrows lifted as she looked at him.

No point in trying to hide his less visible disability now. "It's true," he said, brushing back his hair to show his behind-the-ear hearing aids. "But that doesn't mean you have to take us in." In fact, staying here was the last thing that would work for him.

He'd promised Gerry he'd take care of his son, conceived during the affair Gerry had while married to Lacey. And he'd promised to keep Charlie's parentage a secret from Lacey.

He was glad he could help his friend, sinner though Gerry had been. Charlie needed a reliable father figure, and Lacey needed to maintain her illusions about her husband. It would serve no purpose for her to find out the truth now; it would only hurt her.

Lacey frowned. "I *was* looking to take in another boarder. I was thinking of maybe somebody who worked the three-to-eleven shift at the pretzel factory. They could come home and sleep, and they wouldn't be bothered by my working on the house at all hours."

"That makes sense," he said, relieved. "That would be better."

"But the thing is," she said slowly, "I haven't found anyone, even though I've been advertising for a couple of weeks. If you wanted to..."

Anxiety clawed at him from inside. How was he supposed to handle this? He could throttle Gerry for putting him into this situation. "I... There are some complications. I need to give this some thought." He knew he was being cryptic, but he needed time to figure it all out.

Unfortunately, Nonna wasn't one to accept anything cryptic from her grandchildren. "What complications? What's going on?"

Vito stood, then sat back down again. Nonna was going to have to know about Charlie soon enough. Lacey, too, along with everyone else in town. It would seem weirder if he tried to hide it now. "The thing is," he said, "I'm not alone. I have someone with me."

"Girlfriend? Wife?" Lacey sounded extremely curious.

Nonna, on the other hand, looked disappointed. "You would never get married without letting your *nonna* know," she said, reaching up to pinch his cheek, and then pulling her hand back, looking apologetic. It took him a minute to realize that she'd hesitated because of his scars.

"One of my finished rooms is a double," Lacey said thoughtfully. "But I don't know what your…friend…would think of the mess and the noise."

This was going off the rails. "It's not a girlfriend or wife," he said.

"Then who?" Nonna smacked his arm in a way that reminded him of when he'd been small and misbehaving. "If not a woman, then who?"

Vito drew in a breath. "Actually," he said, "I've recently become certified as a foster parent."

Both women stared at him with wide, surprised eyes.

"So I'd be bringing along my eight-year-old foster son."

He was saved from further explanation by a crash, followed by the sound of shattering glass and running feet.

Chapter Two

Lacey raced out of Nonna's bedroom, leaving Vito to reassure the older woman. A quick scan of the hall revealed the breakage: her ceramic rooster lay in pieces on the floor.

One of the kids, probably; they were all sugared up on wedding cake and running around. She hurried to get a broom and dustpan, not wanting any of the remaining wedding guests to injure themselves. As she dropped the colorful pieces into the trash, she felt a moment's regret.

More important than the untimely demise of her admittedly tacky rooster, she wondered about Vito fostering a child. That, she hadn't expected.

"Miss Lacey!" It was little Mindy, Sam Hinton's daughter. "I saw who did that!"

"Did you? Stay back," she warned as she checked the area for any remaining ceramic pieces.

"Yes," Mindy said, "and he's hiding under the front porch right now!"

Behind her, Lacey heard Vito coming out of Nonna's bedroom, then pausing to talk some more, and a suspicion of who the young criminal might be came over her. "I'll go talk to him," she said. "It wasn't Xavier, was it?"

"No. It was a kid I don't know. Is he going to get in trouble?"

"I don't think so, honey. Not too much trouble, anyway. Why don't you go tell your dad what happened?"

"Yeah! He's gotta know!" As Mindy rushed off to her important task, Lacey walked out of the house and stood on the porch, looking around. The remaining guests were in the side yard, talking and laughing, so no one seemed to notice her.

She went down the steps and around to the side of the house where there was an opening in the latticework; she knew because she'd had to crawl under there when she'd first found Mrs. Whiskers, hiding with a couple of kittens. When she squatted down, she heard a little sniffling sound that touched her heart. Moving aside the branches of a lilac bush, breathing in the sweet fragrance of the fading purple flowers, she spoke into the darkness. "It's okay. I didn't like that rooster much, anyway."

There was silence, and then a stirring, but no voice. From the other side of the yard, she could hear conversations and laughter. But this shaded spot felt private.

"I remember one time I broke my grandma's favorite lamp," she said conversationally, settling into a sitting position on the cool grass. "I ran and hid in an apple tree."

"Did they find you?" a boy's voice asked. Not a familiar voice. Since she knew every kid at the wedding, her suspicion that the culprit was Vito's new foster son increased. "Yes, they found me. My brother told them where I was."

"Did you get in trouble?"

"I sure did." She remembered her grandma's reprimand, her father chiming in, her own teary apology.

"Did they hit you?" the boy asked, his voice low.

The plaintive question squeezed Lacey's heart. "No, I just got scolded a lot. And I had to give my grandma my allowance to help pay for a new lamp."

"I don't get an allowance. Did you…" There was a pause, a sniffle. "Did you have to go live somewhere else after that?"

Lacey's eyes widened as she put it all together. Vito had said he'd *recently* become certified as a foster parent. So this must be a new arrangement. It would make all the sense in the world that a boy who'd just been placed with a new foster father would feel insecure about whether he'd be allowed to stay.

But why had Vito, a single man with issues of his own, taken on this new challenge? "No, I didn't have to go live somewhere else," she said firmly, "and what's more, no kind adult would send a kid away for breaking a silly old lamp. Or a silly old rooster, either."

Branches rustled behind her, and then Vito came around the edge of the bushes. "There you are! What happened? Is everything okay?"

She pointed toward the latticed area where the boy was hiding, giving Vito a meaningful look. "I think the person who *accidentally*—" she emphasized the word "—broke the rooster is worried he'll get sent away."

"What?" Vito's thick dark eyebrows came down as understanding dawned in his eyes. He squatted beside her. "Charlie, is that you? Kids don't get sent away for stuff like that."

There was another shuffling under the porch, and then a head came into view.

Messy, light brown hair, a sprinkling of freckles, worried-looking eyes. "But they might get sent away if they were keeping their dad from having a place to live."

Oh. The boy must have heard Vito say he couldn't live here because of having a foster son.

"We'll find a place to live," Vito said. "Come on out."

The boy looked at him steadily and didn't move.

"Charlie! I mean it!"

Lacey put a hand on Vito's arm. "Hey, Charlie," she said softly. "I grew up next door to this guy. I was three years younger and a lot smaller, and I did some annoying things. And he never, ever hit me." She felt Vito's arm tense beneath hers and squeezed. "And he wouldn't hurt you, either. Right, Vito?" She looked over at him.

His mouth twisted. "That's right." He went forward on one knee and held out a hand to the boy. "Come on out. We talked about this. Remember, I look meaner than I really am."

The boy hesitated, then crawled out without taking Vito's hand. Instead, he scuttled over to the other side of Lacey and crouched.

Vito drew in a breath and blew it out. His brow furrowed. "You're going to need to apologize to Miss Lacey, here, and then we'll find out how you can make up for what you did."

The boy wrapped his arms around upraised knees. A tear leaked out and he backhanded it away. "I can't make it up. Don't have any money."

"I might have some chores you could do," Lacey said, easing backward so she wasn't directly between Charlie and Vito. "Especially if you and your foster dad are going to be living here." As soon as she said it, she regretted the words. "Or living nearby," she amended hastily.

She liked Vito, always had. And she adored his grandmother, who clearly wanted her family gathered around her. But Lacey had been planning to have the next few months as a quiet, calm oasis before opening her guesthouse. She still had healing to do.

Having Vito and this boy here wasn't conducive to quiet serenity. On the other hand, young Charlie seemed to have thrown himself on her for protection, and that touched her.

"Can we live here? Really?" The boy jumped up and started hopping from one foot to the next. "'Cause this place is cool! You have a tire swing! And there's a basketball hoop right across the street!"

Vito stood, looking at her quizzically. "The grown-ups will be doing some talking," he said firmly. "For tonight, we're staying out at the motel like we planned. But before we go back there, I want you to apologize."

The boy looked at Lacey, then away, digging the toe of a well-worn sneaker into the dirt. "I'm real sorry I broke your rooster. It was an accident."

She nodded, getting to her feet. "That's

all right. I think I can find another one kind of like it."

Her own soft feelings surprised her. Generally, she avoided little ones, especially babies; they were a reminder of all she couldn't have.

But this boy touched her heart. Maybe it was because his reaction to breaking the rooster was so similar to her own reaction when she'd broken the lamp. *Hide. Don't let the grown-ups know, because you never know what disaster will happen when grown-ups get upset.* She'd been fortunate, found by her grandma and father instead of her mom. Come to think of it, her brother had probably gone to them on purpose. He'd wanted her to get in trouble, but not from their volatile mother.

Lacey was beyond all that now, at least she thought so, but she still identified with the feeling of accidentally causing disasters and facing out-of-proportion consequences.

"And the other question you have to answer," Vito said, putting an arm around

Charlie's shoulders lightly, ignoring the boy's automatic wince, "is how you got down here when you were supposed to be staying with Valencia."

Lacey moved to stand by Charlie, and her presence seemed to relax him.

"I asked her if we could take a walk," Charlie explained, a defensive tone coming into his voice. "When we came by here, she started talking to the people and I came inside. I just wanted to look around."

"You're not to do things like that without permission." Vito pinched the bridge of his nose. "You have another apology to make, to Valencia. And no dessert after dinner tonight."

The boy's lower lip came out, and Lacey felt the absurd impulse to slip him an extra piece of wedding cake.

An accented voice called from the other side of the yard. "Charlie! Charlie!"

"You run and tell Miss Valencia you're sorry you didn't stay close to her. And then wait for me on the porch."

As the boy ran toward the babysitter's anxious voice, Lacey looked up at Vito. "In over your head?"

"Totally." He blew out a breath. "What do I know about raising kids?"

"How'd you get into it, anyway?"

"It's complicated." He looked away, then back at her. "Listen, don't feel pressured into having us stay at your guesthouse. I don't expect that, no matter what Nonna says. And you can see that we'd be a handful."

She looked into his warm brown eyes. "I *can* see that. And I honestly don't know if it would work. But what are you going to do if you can't stay here?"

"That's the million-dollar question." He rubbed his chin. "We'll figure something out."

"Let me sleep on it. It's been a crazy day."

"Of course it has, and I'm sorry to add to that." They headed toward the rest of the guests, and he put an arm around her shoulders and squeezed. It was an innocent gesture, a friendly gesture, the same thing he'd done with Charlie.

But for some reason, it disconcerted her now, and she stepped away.

Something flashed in Vito's eyes and he cleared his throat. "Look, tomorrow Charlie has a visit with his birth mom up in Raystown. Let me take you to lunch. We can talk about Nonna and the possibility of Charlie and me staying here. Or more likely, how to break it to Nonna that we *won't* be staying here."

She'd planned to spend the next afternoon cleaning up and recovering from the wedding. "That'll work."

"The Chatterbox? Noon?" His voice was strictly businesslike.

"Where else?" She wondered why he'd gone chilly on her. "I'm looking forward to catching up."

And she was. Sort of.

The next morning, Vito pulled his truck into the parking lot at the Supervised Visitation Center and glanced into the backseat of the extended cab. Yes, a storm was brewing.

"Why do I have to do this?" Charlie mumbled. "Am I going back to live with her?"

"No." He twisted farther around to get more comfortable. "We talked about this. Your mom loves you, but she can't do a good job taking care of you, and you need to have a forever home." He'd practically memorized the words from the foster parenting handbook, and it was a good thing. Because apparently, Charlie needed to hear them a bunch of times.

"Then why do I have to visit? I wanted to play basketball with Xavier, that kid from the wedding yesterday. He said maybe I could come over."

Vito pulled up another memorized phrase and forced cheer into his voice. "It's important for you to have a relationship with your mom. Important for you and for her."

The whole situation was awful for a kid, and Krystal, Charlie's mother, wasn't easy to deal with. She'd neglected Charlie, and worse, exposed him to danger—mostly from her poorly chosen boyfriends—way too many times.

Someone who hurt a kid ought to be in prison, in Vito's mind, at the very least. But he had to keep reminding himself that Krystal was sick.

"You'll have fun with your mom," he said. "I think you guys are going to go out for lunch in a little while and maybe over to the lake afterward."

"That doesn't sound fun." Charlie crossed his arms and looked out the window, making no move to get out of the car.

Vito looked that way, too, and saw Krystal getting out of the passenger side of a late-model SUV. Maybe things were looking up for her. He'd only met her a few times, but she'd been driving a car noticeably on its last legs.

The SUV roared off, passing them, with a balding, bearded, forty-something guy at the wheel. Vito looked back at Charlie in time to see the boy cringe. "What's wrong, buddy?" he asked. "Do you know that guy?"

Charlie nodded but didn't say anything.

Krystal strolled over to the back stoop of the Center, smoking a cigarette. Vito wished for a similarly easy way to calm his nerves.

He wished he knew how to be a father. He'd only had Charlie full-time for a month, most of which they'd spent in Cleveland, closing down Vito's previous life, getting ready to move home. Charlie had been well and truly welcomed by the Cleveland branch of Vito's family, though everyone had agreed on waiting to tell Nonna about Charlie until the foster care situation was definite. If everything went well, he'd be able to adopt Charlie after another six months and be the boy's permanent, real father.

Learning how to parent well would take a lifetime.

Vito got out of the car. The small, wire-supported trees around the brand-new building were trying their best, sporting a few green leaves. A robin hopped along the bare ground, poking for worms, and more birds chirped overhead. It was a nice summer day, and Vito was half tempted to get back in the truck and drive away, take Charlie to the lake himself.

But that wasn't the agreement he'd made. He opened the passenger door and Charlie got out. His glance in his mother's direction was urgent and hungry.

Of course. This visit was important. No matter what parents did, kids always wanted to love them.

Vito forced a spring into his step as they approached the building and Krystal. "Hey," he greeted her, and tried the door.

"It's locked, genius." Krystal drew harder on her cigarette. She hadn't glanced at or touched Charlie, who'd stopped a few steps short of the little porch.

Looking at the two of them, Vito's heart about broke. He considered his big, extended family up in Cleveland, the hugs, the cheek pinches, the loud greetings. He had it good, always had. He squatted beside Charlie and cast about for conversation. "Charlie's been doing great," he said to Krystal, not that she'd asked. "Going to sign him up for summer softball."

"Nice for you. I never could afford it." She looked at Charlie then, and her face softened. "Hey, kid. You got tall in the past couple months."

Vito was so close to Charlie that he could sense the boy's urge to run to his mom as well as the fear that pinned him to Vito's side.

The fear worried him.

But Charlie would be safe. This was a supervised visit, if the caseworker ever got here.

"You were Gerry's buddy," Krystal said suddenly. "Did you know about me, or did he just talk about *her*?"

What was Vito supposed to say to that, especially in front of Charlie? The boy needed to think highly of his father, to remember that he'd died a hero's death, not that he'd lived a terribly flawed life. "It's better we focus on now," he said to Krystal, nodding his head sideways, subtly, at Charlie.

She snorted, but dropped the subject, turning away to respond to her buzzing phone.

Focus on now. He needed to take his own advice. Except he had to think about the future and make plans, to consider the possibility of him and Charlie staying with the *her*—Lacey—that Krystal was mad about. Which would be a really rotten idea, now that the ramifications of it all came to him.

He wasn't sure how much Krystal knew about Lacey and Gerry, what kind of promises Gerry might have made to her. From what he'd been able to figure out, Krystal hadn't known that Gerry was married, at least not at first. No wonder she was angry. Problem was, she'd likely pass that anger on to Charlie. She didn't seem like a person who had a very good filter.

And if she talked to Charlie about Lacey, and Charlie was living at Lacey's boarding-house, the boy could get all mixed up inside.

If Gerry were still alive, Vito would strangle him. The jerk hadn't been married to Lacey for a year before he'd started stepping out on her.

Krystal put her phone away, lit another cigarette and sat down on the edge of the stoop. She beckoned to Charlie. "Come on, sit by me. You scared?"

Charlie hesitated, then walked over and sat gingerly beside her. When she put her arm around him, though, he turned into her and hugged her suddenly and hard, and grief tightened her face.

Vito stepped back to give them some space and covertly studied Krystal. He didn't understand Gerry. The man had had Lacey as a wife—gorgeous, sweet Lacey—and he'd cheated on her with Krystal. Who, admittedly, had a stellar figure and long black hair. She'd probably been beautiful back then. But now the hair was disheveled. Her eyes were heavy-lidded, her skin pitted with some kind of scars. Vito wasn't sure what all she was addicted to, but the drugs had obviously taken their toll.

It looked like she'd stayed sober to visit with Charlie today, knowing she'd have to submit to a drug test. Maybe she'd had to stay clean a couple of days. That would put any addict into a bad mood.

Even before she'd been an addict, Krystal couldn't have compared to Lacey.

A battered subcompact pulled into the parking lot and jolted to a halt, its muffler obviously failing. The driver-side door flew open and the short, curly-haired caseworker got out. After pulling an overstuffed brief-case and a couple of bags from her car, she bustled over to them.

"Sorry I'm late! These Sunday visits are crazy. Maybe we can switch to Mondays or Tuesdays?" She was fumbling for the key as she spoke. "Come on in, guys! Thanks so much, Vito!"

"Charlie." Vito got the boy's attention, held his eyes. "I'll be back at three, okay?"

Relief shone on Charlie's face. He ran to Vito, gave him a short hug and whispered into his ear: "Come back for sure, okay?"

"You got it, buddy." Vito's voice choked up a little bit.

Charlie let go and looked at Vito. Then his eyes narrowed and he grinned purposefully. "And can we stay at that place instead of the motel?" he whispered. "With the cat and the nice lady?"

Vito knew manipulation when he saw it, but he also knew the boy needed both security and honesty.

"What's he begging for now?" Krystal grinned as she flicked her cigarette butt into the bare soil beside the building. "I recognize that look."

"I'm starting to recognize it, too," Vito said, meeting Krystal's eyes. Some kind of understanding arced between them, and he felt a moment of kinship and sorrow for the woman who'd given birth to Charlie but wouldn't get to raise him.

"Well, can we?" Charlie asked.

"We'll see. No promises." Vito squeezed the boy's shoulder. "You be good, and I'll see you right here at three o'clock."

In reality, he wished he could just sweep the boy up and take him home, and not just to protect him from an awkward day with his mom. Vito wasn't looking forward to the lunch date—no, *not* a date—he was facing in only a few hours. Whatever he and Lacey decided, it was going to make someone unhappy.

Chapter Three

"They left the two of us in charge of the nursery? Are they crazy?" Lacey's friend Susan put her purse up on a shelf and came over to where Lacey stood beside a crib, trying to coax a baby to sleep.

"I'm just glad it's you working with me." Lacey picked up the baby, who'd started to fuss, and swayed gently. "You won't freak out if I freak out."

Working in the church nursery was Lacey's counselor's idea, a way to help Lacey deal with her miscarriage and subsequent infertility. She needed to desensitize herself, find ways to be around babies without getting upset by them, especially if she was going to open a family-friendly guesthouse and make a success of it.

The desensitization had started accidentally, when Gina Patterson had showed up in town earlier this year with her son, Bobby, just ten months old at the time. With nowhere else to turn, she'd spent the early spring at the guesthouse, in the process falling in love with Lacey's brother, Buck. Being around little Bobby had made Lacey miserable at first, but she was learning. More than that, she was motivated; she wanted to serve others and get out of her own pain, build a well-rounded life for herself.

Which included being around babies. "I'm here to work through my issues," she told Susan, "but why are *you* here?"

Susan's tawny skin went pink. "Sam and I decided it would be a good idea for me to get comfortable with babies. I used to be terrified of even touching them, but… I guess I'd better learn."

Something in Susan's tone made Lacey

take notice, and she mentally reviewed what Susan had just said. Then she stared at her friend. "Wait a minute. Are you expecting? Already?"

Susan looked down at the floor, and then met Lacey's eyes. "Yeah. We just found out."

Selfish tears sprang to Lacey's eyes as she looked down at the infant she held, feeling its weight in her arms. Something she'd never experience for herself, with her own child. A joy that Susan and many of Lacey's other friends would find effortlessly.

Susan would be a part of the circle of happy young mothers in town. Lacey wouldn't, not ever.

"I'm so sorry to cause you pain. News like this must be hard for you to hear."

Susan's kind words jolted Lacey out of her own self-centered heartache. Finding out you were having a baby was one of the most joyous times of a woman's life. She remembered when the two pink lines had shown up on her own pregnancy test. Remembered her video call to Gerry. She'd shown the test to him, and they'd both cried tears of joy.

Susan deserved to have that joy, too. She shouldn't have to focus on her friend's losses.

Lacey lifted the baby to her shoulder so she could reach out and put an arm around Susan. "It does hurt a little—I'm not going to lie. But what kind of friend would I be not to celebrate with you? I'm thrilled!"

"You're the best, Lace." Susan wrapped her arms around Lacey, the baby in between them, and Lacey let herself cry just a little more. Susan understood. She'd stayed a year at Lacey's guesthouse before the remodeling, the horrible year when Lacey had lost both Gerry and the baby. Susan had been an incredible comfort.

"Anyway," Susan added, "I'm going to need your help to fit in with the perfect mothers of Rescue River. You know I have a knack for saying the wrong thing."

"You'll be fine." And it was true. Susan was outspoken and blunt, but she gave everything she had to the kids she taught at the local elementary school, and people here loved her for it. "How's Sam handling the news?"

"Making a million plans and bossing me around, of course." But Susan smiled as she said it, and for just a moment, Lacey felt even more jealous of the happy-married-woman smile on Susan's face than of the tiny, growing baby in her belly.

"Hey, guys, can I leave Bobby here for a little while?" Lou Ann Miller, who was taking care of Gina's baby while she and Buck enjoyed a honeymoon at the shore, stood at the half door. "I want to go to adult Sunday school, but there's no way he'll sit through our book discussion."

"Sure." Lacey thrust the infant she'd been holding into Susan's arms. "Just hold her head steady. Yeah, like that." She walked over to the door and opened it. "Come on in, Bobby!"

"Laaasss," he said, walking right into her leg and hugging it. "Laaasss."

Lacey's heart warmed, and she reached

down to pick Bobby up. "He'll be fine. Take your time," she said to Lou Ann. "Wave bye-bye to Miss Lou Ann, okay?"

Two more toddlers got dropped off, and then a diaper needed changing. Little Emmie Farmingham, who was almost three, twirled to show Lacey and Susan her new summer dress, patterned with garden vegetables and sporting a carrot for a pocket. Then she proceeded to pull the dress off.

Once they'd gotten Emmie dressed again, the infant sleeping and the other two toddlers playing side by side with plastic blocks, Susan and Lacey settled down into the tiny chairs around the low table. "Babies are great, I guess," Susan said doubtfully, "but I have to say, I like bigger kids better. I wish one could just land in my lap at age five, like Mindy did."

"Not me." Lacey looked over at the toddlers, another surge of regret piercing her heart. "I've always loved the little ones."

"I know you have." Susan's voice was gentle. "Hey, want to come over and have lunch with us after this? I think Sam's grilling. You could bring your swimsuit."

"You're sweet." The thought of lounging by Sam and Susan's pool was appealing. And Susan was a great friend; she'd stand by Lacey even as she was going through this huge transition of having a child. She wouldn't abandon Lacey, and that mattered.

Lacey shook her head with real disappointment. "Can't. I'm meeting Vito for lunch."

"Oh, *Vito.*" Susan punched her arm, gently. "Is this a date?"

"It's not like that. We're old friends."

Susan ignored her words. "You should see where it leads. He seems like a great guy, from what I saw of him at the end of the reception. Good-looking, too. Even with the scars." Susan's hand flew to her mouth. "I shouldn't say things like that, should I?"

"Probably not." Lacey rolled her eyes at her friend, pretending exasperation. "But it's okay. You can't help but notice his scars. Anyway, we're just going to talk about this crazy idea his grandma dreamed up." She explained how Nonna had unexpectedly rented out her own house, and how Vito was newly a foster father. "Apparently, Vito had no idea that was her plan. He was counting on bringing his foster son, Charlie, to live in Nonna's big house out in the country. I actually got the feeling Nonna had kept it a secret on purpose, to make sure Vito ended up staying at the guesthouse."

"But that would be perfect!" Susan clapped her hands. "Vito could be with his *nonna*, and Charlie could get a sense of family, and they'd be right in town to get, like, reintegrated into the community."

"Yes, but—"

"And you wanted someone else to room in, right? He'd pay rent, which would help with your expenses. He and Charlie could have separate rooms, or those two connecting ones upstairs."

Lacey's response was cut off by the sound of crashing blocks and a wail, and they got busy playing with the babies. The subject of Vito moving into the guesthouse didn't come up again, but Lacey couldn't stop thinking about it.

Susan seemed to think it was a great idea, and Nonna had talked to Lacey over breakfast about how wonderful it would be to have Vito there and to get to know the newest member of the family. Her eyes had sparkled when she said that, and few enough things had brought a sparkle to Nonna's eyes since the heart attack.

There were all kinds of reasons to embrace the idea of Vito and Charlie moving in, but Lacey still felt uneasy about it.

She couldn't begin to articulate why, even to herself.

At lunchtime, Vito stood outside the Chatterbox Café, looking up at the town's outdoor clock, which clearly showed it was only eleven forty-five. He was early. Why had he come so early?

He loosened the itchy collar of his new button-down shirt. He shouldn't have worn a brand-new shirt today, should have at least washed it first, except that he was living out of a suitcase and he'd been rushing to get Charlie ready to go and there hadn't been the chance.

He could have just worn an old, comfortable shirt, but the fact was, he was trying to look good. Which was obviously a losing battle.

It wasn't about Lacey. It was about the fact that he'd probably see other people he knew here at the Chatterbox, and he needed to present a professional image. He had good benefits from the VA—they were paying for his online degree—but a man needed to work, and Vito would be looking for a part-time job just as soon as he'd found a place to live and gotten Charlie settled. Maybe something with kids, since he was looking to become a teacher.

No, it wasn't about Lacey. He'd had some feelings for her once, but he'd turned those off when she'd married, of course. He'd been over her for years.

"Vito!" Lacey approached, a summery

yellow dress swirling around her legs, the wind blowing her short hair into messiness.

She looked so beautiful that, for a moment, he couldn't breathe.

He crooked his arm for her to take it, an automatic gesture he'd learned at his *nonna*'s knee. The way a gentleman treated a lady. And then he remembered how she'd stepped away when he'd done the Italian thing and thrown an arm around her yesterday. He put his arm back at his side.

People are disgusted by your scars, he reminded himself. *And she hasn't seen the half of them.*

As they turned toward the café—Vito carefully *not* touching her—he caught a whiff of something lemony and wondered if it was her shampoo, or if she'd worn perfume.

Inside, everything was familiar: the smell of meat loaf and fries, the red vinyl booths and vintage tables trimmed with aluminum, the sight of people he'd known since childhood. Even the counter waitress, Nora Jean, had been here since he was a kid and called a greeting.

"Sit anywhere, you two. Lindy'll wait on you, but I'm coming over to say hello just as soon as these guys give me a break." She waved at her full counter.

Dion Coleman, the police chief, swiveled in his chair and stood to pound Vito on the back. "I'm glad to see your ugly mug," he joked. Which didn't feel awkward, because it was the exact same thing Dion had always said when Vito came home, even before his injuries. "Police business has been slow these past months, but with you home, it's sure to pick up."

Vito shook the man's hand with genuine pleasure. "I'll see what I can do about knocking down some mailboxes and shooting up signs, just to give you something to do. You're getting soft." He nodded down at Dion's flat belly and then at the grilled chicken salad on the counter in front of him. "Eating too much. Just like a cop."

"You never change." Dion was laughing

as he sat back down. "Give me a call, you hear? We have some catching up to do."

Lacey had headed toward one of the few empty booths at the back of the café, and as he followed her it seemed to Vito that conversation stopped, then rose again when he'd passed. He rubbed a hand across his face, feeling the uneven ridges of his scars.

As soon as they sat down, they were mobbed. The young waitress could barely squeeze in to take their order. Everyone, friend or acquaintance, stopped by to say hello. They wanted to know where he was staying, how long he'd be in town, where he was stationed. Explaining that he wasn't in the army anymore felt embarrassing, since he'd always intended it to be his life's work. More embarrassing were the sympathetic nods and arm pats. People felt sorry for him.

But he kept it upbeat and answered questions patiently. Once people knew his story, they'd settle down some. And maybe someone would think of him when a job opening came up, so he made sure to let everyone know he was looking.

After people had drifted back to their tables and they'd managed to eat some of their lunch, Lacey wiped her mouth and smiled at him. "That got a little crazy. Are you wishing we'd gone somewhere else?"

He swallowed his massive bite of cheeseburger and shook his head. "Best to get it over fast. Let people get a good look."

She took a sip of soda. "You think they all came over to look at your scars?"

"That, and find out the latest news. But mostly to see how bad the damage is, up close and personal." His support group at the VA had warned him about people's reactions, how they might not be able to see anything but his scars at first.

"They're not looking at your scars in a bad way," Lacey said, frowning. "They're grateful for your service."

Of course, that was what most of the people who'd greeted them had said. And they weren't lying. It was just that initial cringe that got to him. He wasn't used to scaring people just by the way he looked.

His friend with severe facial burns had told Vito that you never really got used to it. "Older people do better, but young people like pretty," he'd said. "Makes it a challenge to get a date."

The waitress refilled his coffee cup and headed to a booth across the way. Vito gestured toward her. "You can't tell me someone like that, someone who doesn't know me, isn't disgusted when she first sees me."

Lacey looked at him for a long moment, her brown eyes steady. "Look over there," she said, pointing to a twenty-something man in an up-to-date wheelchair, sitting at a table with an older woman. "That's our waitress's brother," she said. "He served, too."

Vito blinked and looked more closely, seeing how the man's head lolled to one side, held up by a special support. He wore a hoodie and sweats, and as Vito watched, the older woman put a bite of something into his mouth.

"Wounded in service?"

Lacey nodded. "I think he was a Marine."

"Is a Marine," Vito corrected. "And I'm sorry. You're right. I need to get out of my own head. I'm more fortunate than a lot of guys." He met her eyes. "Gerry included, and I'm a jerk to focus on myself."

She shrugged. "We all do that sometimes."

Had Lacey always had this steady maturity? He couldn't help but remember her as a younger girl, pestering him and her brother when they'd wanted to go out and do something fun. And he remembered how flightily she'd fallen for Gerry, swept away by love and unable to listen to anyone's warnings.

Now though, there was real thoughtfulness to her. She was quieter than she'd been, and more assertive.

He liked that. Liked a woman who'd call him on his dumb mistakes.

And he didn't need to be thinking about how much he liked the new Lacey. Best to get to the real reason for their lunch. "So, I was looking into options for Charlie and me," he said. "I talked to the family Nonna rented her house to."

"And? Did you ask if they'd let her out of the contract?"

"I couldn't even bring it up." He lifted his hands, shrugging. "They're thrilled with the house and the price Nonna gave them, and they need the space. And she's pregnant out to here." He held a hand in front of his stomach.

"Well, look who's back in town!" Old Mr. Love from the hardware store, who had to be in his eighties, stopped by their table and patted his shoulder. "I'd recognize that voice anywhere!"

Vito stood and greeted the man, and then looked at the gray-haired woman with him. "Miss Minnie Falcon? Is that you?"

"That's right, young man. You'd better not forget your old Sunday school teacher."

"I couldn't ever forget." He took her hand, gently. Unlike some of the other kids in Sunday school, he'd actually appreciated Miss Minnie's knowledge of the Old and New

Testament, and the way she brought the stories to life, infusing them with a sense of biblical history.

Mr. Love was leaning toward Lacey. "I was hoping you'd find romance." His voice, meant to be low, carried clearly to Vito and Miss Minnie. "Now that Buck's out of your hair, it's your turn, young lady." He nodded toward Vito, raising an eyebrow.

"Harold!" Miss Minnie scolded. "Don't make assumptions. Come on. Let's get that corner table before someone else takes it." She patted Vito's arm. "It was nice to see you. Don't be a stranger. We like visitors over at the Senior Towers." She turned and headed across the restaurant at a brisk pace, pushing her wheeled walker.

"When a lady talks, you listen." Mr. Love gave Vito an apologetic shrug as he turned and followed Miss Minnie, putting a hand on her shoulder.

After they were out of earshot, Vito lifted an eyebrow at Lacey. "They're a couple?"

"It's anybody's guess. They both say they're

just friends, but tongues are wagging. It *is* Rescue River."

"Gossip central," he agreed, sipping coffee.

"And speaking of wagging tongues," she said, "imagine what people will assume about us if you come and live in the guesthouse. Just like Mr. Love assumed when he saw us together here. They'll think *we're* a couple. And I'm not comfortable with that."

"I understand." He looked down at his hands, traced a scar that peeked out from his shirt cuff. "I'm not exactly a blue-ribbon bronco."

"Vito!" She sounded exasperated. "You haven't changed a bit since you had to try on six different shirts for the homecoming dance."

The memory made him chuckle. He'd gotten her to sit on the porch and judge while he tried on shirt after shirt, running back to his room to change each time she'd nixed his selection.

Little did she know that Buck had begged

him to keep her busy while he tried to steal a few kisses from cheerleader Tiffany Townsend, ostensibly at their house for help with homework.

"That was a long time ago," he said now. "And the truth is, I *have* changed."

She rolled her eyes. "You're still good-looking, okay? Women don't mind scars." Then she pressed her lips together as her cheeks grew pink.

His heart rate accelerated, just a little. Why was she blushing? Did *she* think he was good-looking?

But of course, she hadn't seen the worst of his scars.

And even if there *was* a little spark between them, it couldn't go anywhere. Because he was living with a secret he couldn't let her discover.

"Look," she said, and then took a big gulp of soda. "Getting back to the idea of you and Charlie staying at the guesthouse. I'd be willing to consider it, for Nonna's sake, but… I'm trying to build a rich, full life as a single person, see, and I don't want everyone asking me questions or trying to match us up. I'm just getting over being Lacey, the pitiful widow. And now, if I have this good-looking man living in my guesthouse..." A flush crept up her cheeks again and she dropped her head, propping her forehead on her hand. "I'm just digging myself in deeper here, huh?"

She *did* think he was good-looking. All of a sudden, other people's curious stares didn't bother him half as much.

"Can I get you anything else?" The perky waitress was back, looking at Lacey with curiosity. "You okay, Lacey?"

"I need something chocolate," she said, looking up at the waitress but avoiding Vito's eyes.

"Right away! I totally understand!"

Vito didn't get women's obsession with chocolate, but he respected it. He waited until the server had brought Lacey a big slice of chocolate cream pie before blundering forward with their meeting's purpose.

"I have an appointment tonight to talk to a woman who might want to rent me a couple of rooms in her farmhouse, out past the dog rescue. And there's the top floor of a house available over in Eastley."

"That's good, I guess." She toyed with the whipped cream on her pie. "But Nonna won't like having you so far away. And Charlie could make more friends in town, right?"

"He really took a shine to the place and to you, it's true."

"And Nonna wants you to live there. She pulled out all the stops at breakfast, trying to talk me into it again."

"She phoned me, too."

Lacey was absently fingering the chain around her neck, and when he looked more closely, he saw what hung on it.

A man's wedding ring. Undoubtedly Gerry's.

He wasn't worth it, Lace.

A shapely blonde in a tight-fitting dress approached their table. Tiffany Townsend.

"Well, Vito D'Angelo. Aren't *you* a sight for sore eyes."

He snorted. "No." And then he thought about what Lacey had said: *Women don't mind scars*. And nobody, even a less-than-favorite classmate like Tiffany, deserved a rude response. He pasted on a smile. "Hey, Tiffany. It's been a long time."

"Where are you hiding yourself these days?" She bent over the table, and Vito leaned back in the booth, trying to look anywhere but down her low-cut dress. "We should get together sometime!" she gushed, putting a hand on his arm.

This was where a suave man would smile and flirt and make a date. But Vito had never been suave. He'd always been the one to console the girls whose boyfriends got caught on Tiffany's well-baited line. Always the friend, happy to take them out for coffee or a milk shake and to listen to them.

Unfortunately for his love life, it hadn't usually gone further than that.

Tiffany was looking at him expectantly. "Where did you say you're staying?"

"I'm not really..." He broke off. Did he really want to get into his personal business with Tiffany?

Lacey cleared her throat, grasped Vito's scarred hand and smiled up at Tiffany. "He's staying at my guesthouse," she said sweetly. "With me."

"Oh." There was a world of meaning in that word, backed up by Tiffany's raised eyebrows. "Well, then. It was good to see you." She spun on her high heels and walked over to the counter, where she leaned toward Nora Jean and started talking fast and hard.

Vito turned his hand over, palm to palm with Lacey. "Thanks," he said, "but you didn't have to do that."

"Tiffany hasn't changed a bit since high school," Lacey said. "She'd break your heart."

"It's not in the market."

"Mine, either."

They looked at each other and some electrical-like current materialized between them, running from their locked eyes to their intertwined hands.

No, Vito's heart wasn't in the market. He had enough to do to rebuild a life and raise a boy and keep a secret.

But if it *had* been in the market, it would run more toward someone like Lacey than toward someone like Tiffany.

Lacey glanced toward the counter. "Don't look now," she said, "but Tiffany and Nora Jean are staring at us."

"This is how rumors get started." He squeezed her hand a little, then could have kicked himself. Was he flirting? With the one woman he could never, ever get involved with?

"That's true," Lacey said briskly, looking away. "And we've obviously done a good job of starting a rumor today. So…"

"So what?" He squeezed her hand again, let go and thought of living at the guesthouse with Nonna and Charlie.

Charlie could walk to the park, or better

yet, ride a bike. Vito was pretty sure there was one in Nonna's garage that he could fix up.

Vito could see Nonna every day. Do something good for the woman who'd done so much for him.

And he could get back on his feet, start his online classes. Maybe Nonna, as she got better, would watch Charlie for him some, giving him a chance to go out and find a decent job.

Soon enough, Nonna would be well and Charlie would be settled in school and Vito would have some money to spare. At which point he could find them another place to live.

He'd only have to keep his secret for the summer. After that, he and Charlie would live elsewhere and would drift naturally out of Lacey's circle of friends. At that point, it was doubtful that she'd learn about Charlie's parentage; there'd be no reason for it to come up.

How likely was it that Lacey would find out the truth over the summer?

"Maybe you could stay for a while," she said. "I'm opening the guesthouse this fall, officially, but until then, having a long-term guest who didn't mind noise would help out."

"How about a guest who makes noise? Charlie's not a quiet kid."

"I liked him."

"Well, then," Vito said, trying to ignore the feeling that he was making a huge mistake, "if you're seriously making the offer, it looks like you've got yourself a couple of tenants for the summer."

Chapter Four

The next Wednesday afternoon, Lacey looked out the kitchen window as Charlie and Vito brought a last load of boxes in from Vito's pickup. Pop music played loudly—Charlie's choice. She'd heard their good-natured argument earlier. The bang of the front screen door sent Mr. Whiskers flying from his favorite sunning spot on the floor. He disappeared into the basement, where his companion, Mrs. Whiskers, had already retreated.

Some part of Lacey liked the noise and life, but part of her worried. There went her peaceful summer—and Nonna's, too. This might be a really bad idea.

She glanced over at the older woman, relaxing in the rocking chair Lacey had put in a warm, sunny corner beside the stove. Maybe she'd leave the chair there. It gave the room a cozy feel. And Nonna didn't look any too disturbed by the ruckus Vito and Charlie were creating. Her eyes sparkled with more interest than she'd shown in the previous couple of weeks.

"I'd better get busy with dinner." Lacey opened the refrigerator door and studied the contents.

"I used to be such a good cook," Nonna commented. "Nowadays, I just don't have the energy."

"You will again." Lacey pulled mushrooms, sweet peppers and broccoli from the fridge. "You'd better. I don't think I could face the future without your lasagna in it."

"I could teach you to make it."

Lacey chuckled. "I'm really not much of a cook. And besides, we need to work on healthy meals. Maybe we can figure out a way to make some heart-healthy lasagna one of these days."

As she measured out brown rice and started it cooking, she looked over to see Nonna's frown. "What's wrong?"

"What are you making?"

"Stir-fried veggies on brown rice. It'll be good." Truthfully, it was one of Lacey's few staples, a quick, healthy meal she often whipped up for herself after work.

"No meat?" Nonna sounded scandalized. "You can't serve a meal to men without meat. At least a little, for flavor."

Lacey stopped in the middle of chopping the broccoli into small florets. "I'm cooking for men?"

"Aren't you fixing dinner for Vito and Charlie, too?" Nonna's eyebrows lifted.

"We didn't talk about sharing meals." Out the window, she saw Vito close the truck cab and wipe his forehead with the back of his hand before picking up one of the street side boxes to carry in. "They *are* working up a sweat out there, but where would I put them?" She nodded toward the small wooden table against the wall, where she and Nonna had been taking their meals. Once again, she sensed their quiet, relaxing summer dissolving away.

At the same time, Nonna was an extrovert, so maybe having more people around would suit her. As for Lacey, she needed to get used to having people in the house, to ease into hosting a bed-and-breakfast gradually, rather than waiting until she had a houseful of paying guests to feed in her big dining room. And who better than good old Vito?

"There's always room for more around a happy home's table," Nonna said, rocking.

"I guess we *could* move it out from the wall."

Vito walked by carrying a double stack of boxes, and Lacey hurried to the kitchen door. "Are you okay with that? Do you need help?" Though from the way his biceps stretched the sleeves of his white T-shirt, he was most definitely okay.

"There's nothing wrong with me below the neck." He sounded uncharacteristically irritable. "I can carry a couple of boxes."

Where had *that* come from? She lifted her hands and took a step back. "Fine with me," she said sharply.

From above them on the stairs, Charlie crowed, "Ooo-eee, a fight!"

Vito ignored him and stomped up the stairs, still carrying both boxes.

"You come in here, son." Nonna stood behind Lacey, beckoning to Charlie.

Lacey bit her lip. She didn't want Nonna to overexert herself. And being from an earlier generation, she might have unreasonable expectations of how a kid like Charlie would behave.

But Nonna was whispering to Charlie, and they both laughed, and then he helped her back to her rocking chair. That was good.

Lacey went back to her cutting board, looked at the stack of veggies and reluctantly acknowledged to herself that Nonna was probably right. If she could even get a red-blooded man and an eight-year-old boy to eat stir-fry, the least she could do was put some beef in it. She rummaged through her refrigerator and found a pack of round steak, already cut into strips. Lazy woman's meat. She drizzled oil into the wok, let it heat a minute, and then dumped in the beef strips.

"Hey, Lace." It was Vito's deep voice, coming from the kitchen doorway. "C'mere a minute."

She glanced around. The rice was cooking, Nonna and Charlie were still talking quietly and the beef was barely starting to brown. She wiped her hands on a kitchen towel. "What's up?" she asked as she crossed the kitchen toward him. "You're not going to bite my head off again, are you?"

"No." He beckoned her toward the front room, where they could talk without the others hearing. "Look, I'm sorry I snapped. Charlie's been a handful and…" He trailed off and rubbed the back of his neck.

"And what?"

"And… I hate being treated like there's something wrong with me. I'm still plenty strong."

"I noticed." But she remembered a similar feeling herself, after her miscarriage; people had tiptoed around her, offering to carry her groceries and help her to a seat in church. When really, she'd been just fine physically. "I'm sorry, too, then. I know how annoying it is to be treated like an invalid."

"So we're good?" He put an arm around her.

It was a gesture as natural as breathing to Vito as well as to the rest of his Italian family. She'd always liked that about them.

But now, something felt different about Vito's warm arm around her shoulders. Maybe it was that he was so much bigger and brawnier than he'd been as a younger man.

Disconcerted, she hunched her shoulders and stepped away.

Some emotion flickered in his eyes and

was gone, so quickly she wasn't sure she'd seen it.

"Hi!" Charlie came out of the kitchen, smiling innocently. He sidestepped toward Nonna's room.

"Where you headed, buddy?" Vito asked.

"Lacey, dear," Nonna called from the kitchen. "I'd like to rest up a little before dinner."

"I'm glad she called me." Lacey heard herself talking a little faster than usual, heard a breathless sound in her own voice. "I try to walk with her, because I have so many area rugs and the house can be a bit of an obstacle course. But of course, she likes to be independent." Why was she blathering like she was nervous, around Vito?

"I'll help her." Vito went into the kitchen and Lacey trailed behind. "Come on, Nonna, I'll walk with you. Smells good," he added, glancing over to where the beef sizzled on the stove.

It *did* smell good, and the praise from Vito

warmed her. She added in sliced mushrooms and onions.

For a moment, all she could hear was the slight sizzle of the food on the stove and the tick of the big kitchen clock on the wall. Peace and quiet. Maybe this was going to work out okay.

The quiet didn't last long. From Nonna's room, she could hear Charlie talking, telling some story. Vito's deeper voice chimed in. His comfortable, familiar laugh tickled her nerve endings in a most peculiar way. Then she heard his heavy step on the stairs. No doubt he was going up to do a little more unpacking while Charlie was occupied. Vito was a hard worker.

And just why was she so conscious of him? What was wrong with her?

She walked over to the sink and picked up the photo she kept on a built-in wooden shelf beside it. Gerry, in uniform, arriving home on one of his furloughs. Someone had snapped a photo of her hugging him, her hair, longer then, flying out behind her, joy in every muscle of her body.

She clasped the picture close to her chest. *That* was reality.

Reassured, she moved out the table and located some chairs for Charlie and Vito, almost wishing Buck hadn't taken her bigger kitchen table with him when he'd moved. She checked on the dinner. Just about done. She found grapes and peaches to put in a nice bowl, both a centerpiece and a healthy dessert.

"What's going on here?" She heard Vito's voice from Nonna's room a little later. He must have come back downstairs. She hadn't even noticed. Good.

Charlie's voice rose, then Nonna's. It sounded like an argument, and Lacey's patient shouldn't be arguing. She wiped her hands and hurried to check on Nonna.

When she looked into the room, both Nonna and Charlie had identical guilty expressions. And identical white smudges on their faces. Beside Nonna was a box from the bakery that someone had brought over yesterday. Cannoli.

"Dessert before dinner, Charlie?" Vito was shaking his head. "You know that's not allowed."

"Nonna!" Lacey scolded. "Rich, heavy pastries aren't on your diet. You know the doctor's worried about your blood sugar."

"She told me where they were and asked me to get them for her," Charlie protested. "And you told me I was supposed to treat older people with respect."

Vito blew out a sigh. "You just need to check with me first, buddy. And Nonna, you've got to stick to your eating plan. It's for your health!"

"What's life without cannoli?" Nonna said plaintively. "Do I have to give up all my treats?"

Vito knelt beside his grandmother. "I think you can have a few planned treats. But sneaking cannoli before dinner means you won't have an appetite for the healthy stuff."

"I didn't anyway," Nonna muttered.

"Me, either." Charlie went to stand beside Nonna on the other side. Obviously, he'd made a new friend in Nonna, and that was all to the good for both of them—as long as it didn't lead to Nonna falling off the diet bandwagon.

It was up to Lacey to be firm, so she marched over and picked up the bakery box. "Whatever you men don't eat for dessert is getting donated tonight," she said firmly. "Obviously, it's too much of a temptation to have things like this in the house."

An acrid smell tickled her nose.

"What's that burning?" Vito asked at the same moment.

"Dinner!" Lacey wailed and rushed into the kitchen, where smoke poured from the rice pan. In the wok, the beef and vegetables had shrunk down and appeared to be permanently attached to the wok's surface.

All her work to make dinner nice and healthy, gone to waste.

She turned off the burners and stared at the ruined food, tears gathering in her eyes.

In her head she could hear her mother's criticism of the cookies she'd baked: *you'll never be much of a chef, will you?*

She remembered Gerry shoving away his dinner plate the first night they'd come back from their honeymoon, saying he wasn't hungry.

Nonna was calling questions from her room and Charlie shouted back: "Lacey burned up dinner!"

The acrid smoke stung her eyes, and then the smoke detector went off with an earsplitting series of beeps.

This was not the serene life she had been looking for. She was a failure as a cook.

She burst into tears.

Vito coughed from the smoke and winced from the alarm's relentless beeping. He turned down the volume on his hearing aids and moved toward Lacey, his arms lifting automatically to comfort her with a hug.

She clung on to him for one precious second, then let go and looked around like she didn't know what to do next.

He needed to take charge. He shut off the smoke detectors, one after the other. Then he opened all the windows in the kitchen, gulping in big breaths of fresh air.

Lacey flopped down at the kitchen table, wiping tears. He beckoned to Charlie. "Run and tell Nonna everything's fine, but dinner will be a little late." As Charlie left the room, Vito scraped the ruined food into the garbage and filled the two pans halfway with soapy water. They'd need some serious scrubbing later.

Lacey was sniffling now, blowing her nose and wiping her eyes.

He leaned back against the counter and studied her. "How come this got you so upset? You're not a crier."

She laughed. "I am, these days. And I'm also a loser in the kitchen, in case you didn't notice. My mom always told me that, and Gerry concurred."

"Gerry?" That was a surprise. The man

had eaten enough MREs in the military that he should have been grateful for any home cooking, however simple.

She pushed herself to her feet. "What'll we eat now? Nonna needs dinner. We all do. I guess, maybe, pizza? But that's not the healthiest choice for your grandma."

"Do you have canned tomatoes?" Vito asked her. "Onions? Garlic? Pasta?"

She nodded and blew her nose again. "I think so."

"Great. You sit down and I'll give you stuff to chop. I'm going to make a spaghetti sauce." He might not know what words to say to comfort her, but he could definitely cook her a meal.

"Spaghetti!" Charlie yelled, pumping his fist as he ran into the kitchen.

"That's right." Vito stepped in front of the racing boy. "And you, young man, are going to do some chores. Starting with taking out this garbage."

Charlie started to protest, but Vito just pointed at the garbage can. Charlie yanked out the bag and stomped out of the house with it.

Lacey chopped and Vito opened cans of tomatoes and set the sauce to cooking. As the onions sizzled in olive oil, the day's tension rolled off him. When Charlie came back in, he had Gramps Camden, a weathered-looking, gray-haired man, with him.

Lacey gave the older man a hug, then turned to Vito. "You remember Gramps Camden, don't you?"

Vito stood and greeted the older man, who'd been a part of the community as long as he could remember.

"Wanted to pay a visit," he said in his trademark grouchy way. "See what you've got going on over here."

"You'll stay for dinner, won't you?" Lacey asked.

"Twist my arm," the old man said. "Cooking's good over at the Senior Towers, but nothing beats homemade."

Lacey asked Charlie to take a couple of

bills out to the mailbox, and he went happily enough.

A knock came on the back screen door, and there was Gina, the woman Lacey's brother, Buck, had married, holding a toddler by the hand. "Hey, Lace, are you in there?"

"C'mon in." Lacey got up and opened the door for the woman, a rueful smile on her face. "Welcome to the zoo."

"Hey," Gina greeted Vito and Gramps Camden, and then turned to Lacey, holding the little boy by his shoulders as he attempted to toddle away. "Can you watch Bobby for ten or fifteen minutes? I have to run over to the Senior Towers to check out a few facts."

Vito's curiosity must have shown on his face, because she explained. "I'm doing some research on the town and the guesthouse. This place was a stop on the Underground Railroad and has a really amazing history."

"Laaaaas," the little boy said, walking into Lacey's outstretched arms.

"Hey, how's my sweet boy?" Lacey wrapped the child in a giant hug, and then stood, lifting him to perch on her hip. Her bad mood was apparently gone. "Look, Bobby, this is Vito. And this is Mr. Camden. Can you say hi?"

Bobby buried his face in Lacey's neck.

"Taking off," Gina said, and hurried out the back door.

Lacey cuddled the little boy close, nuzzling his neck, and then brought him to the window. "Look at the birdies," she said, pointing toward a feeder outside the window where a couple of goldfinches fluttered.

"Birdie," Bobby agreed.

"You're a natural," Vito said, meaning it. Lacey looked right at home with a child in her arms, and the picture made a longing rise in him. He wanted a baby. More than one.

And Lacey probably needed to have another baby. It would help her get over the pain of her devastating miscarriage.

Lacey set the table, having Bobby bring

napkins along to help, letting him place them haphazardly on the table and chairs.

Vito tasted the sauce and frowned. "It needs something."

"I have basil growing outside. At least, I *think* it's still alive. Want some?"

"Fresh basil? For sure."

"Come on, Bobby." She helped the little boy maneuver across the kitchen and through the back door.

Could Vito be blamed for looking out the window to see where her herbs were planted? After all, he might do more cooking here. He was enjoying it.

And once he looked, and saw her kneeling in the golden late-afternoon sunlight, pointing and talking with Bobby, he found it hard to look away.

"Take a picture, it lasts longer," Gramps muttered. "Do I have to chaperone everyone around here?"

Vito blinked and went back to his cooking, but the image of Lacey, the curve of her neck, soft hair blowing in the breeze, stayed with him.

Who was he to think romantically about someone so beautiful, so perfect?

Half an hour later, they were about to sit down to a not-bad-looking dinner when Gina tapped on the back door.

"Mama!" Bobby cried and toddled toward the door.

She opened the door, scooped up her son and gave him a big loud kiss.

"You'll stay for dinner, won't you?" Lacey asked Gina.

"Oh…no. I would but… I need to get home." Her cheeks went pink and Vito put it together. She was a new bride, must have just gotten back from a brief honeymoon. She wanted to get home to her new husband.

Envy tugged at Vito's heart. Would he ever have a wife who was eager to return to him, or would he always remain just the best friend?

Dinner was fun. Nonna insisted they put on some Italian opera music—"the most romantic music on earth!"—and then got into a good-natured argument with Gramps

Camden, who insisted that Frank Sinatra sang the best love songs. Her eyes sparkled with pleasure as everyone talked and joked and ate. Charlie enjoyed the company, too. Both of them would benefit from being part of a bigger family, Vito realized. He would, as well.

He just didn't know how to make it happen. But at least for the summer, it was something they could enjoy here at Lacey's. He would talk to her about having meals together as often as possible, splitting grocery bills and sharing cooking duties.

When he stood to clear the dishes, Lacey put a hand on his arm. "It's okay, Vito. You cooked, so I'll clean up."

"It's a lot," he protested, trying not to notice the delicate feel of her hand.

"I have an excellent helper," she said, letting go of Vito and patting Charlie's arm. "Right?"

"Sure," the boy said with surprising good cheer.

Of course. Lacey had that effect on every

male of the species. Her charm wasn't meant specially for him.

"You can walk me back over to the Towers," Gramps said unexpectedly to Vito, so after a few minutes of parting conversation, the two of them headed down to the street. The Towers were almost next door to Lacey's guesthouse, and Gramps seemed plenty strong to get there on his own, but maybe he just wanted the company. Fine with Vito. He needed to get away from pretty Lacey, get some fresh air.

"How you handling those scars?" Gramps asked abruptly.

Vito felt the heat rise up his neck and was glad for the darkness and the cool breeze. "Apart from terrifying women and children, no big deal."

Gramps chuckled. "It's what's on the inside that counts. Any woman worth her salt will know that. The kid over there seems like he gets it, too."

It was true; the few occasions Charlie still cringed away from Vito had more to do with leftover fears related to his mother's boyfriends than with Vito's looks.

They were almost to the front door of the Towers now, and Vito was ready to say goodbye when Gramps stopped and turned toward him. "Just what are your intentions toward Lacey?"

Vito pulled back to stare at the older man. "Intentions?"

"That's right. Some of us over at the Towers got to talking. Wondered whether you and she had more than a landlord-tenant friendship."

"Hey, hey now." Vito held up a hand. "Nobody needs to be gossiping about Lacey. She's had enough trouble in her life already."

Gramps propped a hand on the railing beside the door. "Don't you think we know that? For that matter, you have, too. The both of you have— What is it young folks call it?"

"Baggage," Vito said. "And we may be young compared to...some people, but we're not so young we need to be told what to do."

Gramps snorted. "Think you know everything, do you?"

"No. Not everything. Not much. But I do know my love life's my business, just as Lacey's love life is hers."

"Give it some thought before you mingle them together, that's all. I'd hate to see either Lacey or that boy hurt."

"I'd hate to see that, too." Vito lifted an eyebrow. "We done here?"

"We're done," Gramps said, "but have a care how you spend the rest of your evening over there."

And even though he found the warning annoying, Vito figured it was probably a wise one.

Chapter Five

When Vito walked back into the guesthouse, he heard dishes clattering in the kitchen. Lacey. Like a magnet, she drew him.

And maybe Gramps knew just what he was talking about. Being careful was the goal Vito needed to shoot for. A vulnerable woman and a vulnerable child were both somewhat under his protection, and Gramps didn't know the half of how any relationship between Lacey and Vito could cause damage to both of them.

He'd expected to see Charlie in the kitchen, but when he got there Lacey was alone, squatting to put away a pan.

"Hey," he said softly, not wanting to startle her. "Where's Charlie?"

She stood and turned toward him. "I told him he could watch TV. He was a good helper, but apparently, it's time for one of his favorite shows."

"Oh, right." Vito should go. He should go right upstairs, right now.

But in the soft lamplight, he couldn't look away from her.

She was looking at him, too, her eyes wide and confused.

He took a step toward her.

Leaning against the counter with one hip, she picked up a framed photo from the counter, studied it for a few seconds, and then placed it carefully on the shelf beside the sink.

"What's that?" He walked over but stopped a good three feet away from her. A safe distance.

She picked it back up and held it out for him to see. "It was Gerry's second time home on furlough. I'd missed him so much that when he came off the plane, I broke away from the other wives and ran screaming to hug him. Somebody caught it on film."

Vito studied the picture of Lacey and his friend, and his heart hurt. They *did* look happy, thrilled to see each other. "Could've been in the newspaper. Good picture."

"It was in the *Plain Dealer*," she said, smiling shyly. "That embarrassed Gerry. Me, too, a little. Everyone kept coming up to us to say they'd seen it."

"Gerry didn't like that, huh?" Vito felt sick inside, because he knew why.

Gerry had already been involved with Krystal at that point. Maybe she'd even been pregnant with Charlie. He thought about asking Lacey the year, and then didn't. He didn't even want to know.

How awkward for Gerry that his girlfriend might see his loving wife hugging on him.

Gerry had been such a jerk.

"He was everything I ever wanted," Lacey

said dreamily, studying the picture. "Sometimes I don't think I'll ever get over him."

"Right. Look, I'd better go check on Charlie and catch some sleep myself." He turned and walked out of the room. An abrupt departure might be a little rude, but it was better than staying there, listening to her express her adoration of a man who'd not been worth one ounce of it. Better than blurting out something that would destroy that idealized image she had of Gerry.

Don't speak ill of the dead. It was a common maxim, and valid.

Was he making a huge mistake to stay here, even though that was what Nonna and Charlie both wanted?

He scrubbed a hand across his face and headed up the stairs. He needed to focus on his professional goals and forget about his personal desire to have a wife and a large family. He needed to make sure that personal desire didn't settle on Lacey, like Gramps seemed to worry it would.

He and Charlie were living in the home

of the one woman he could never, ever be involved with. He'd promised Gerry at the moment of his death, and that meant something. It meant a lot. The sooner he got that straight in his head, the better.

On Friday, Lacey strolled along the sidewalk with Vito and Charlie and tried to shake the odd feeling that they were a family, doing errands together. It was a strange thought, especially given that her goal was to get her guesthouse up and running so that she could dive into her self-sufficient, single-woman life and make it good.

She just needed to keep in mind the purpose of this trip: to create a cozy room at the guesthouse for any child who came to stay for a night or a weekend.

It was only midafternoon, but with the arrival of summer, a lot of people seemed to be taking off work early on Fridays. A group of women clustered outside of the Chatterbox Café, talking. A young couple pushed their baby in a stroller. Several people she knew vaguely from the Senior Towers were taking their afternoon walk, and outside Chez la Ferme, Rescue River's only fancy restaurant, Sam Hinton stood with sleeves rolled up, talking to another man in a suit, smiling like he'd just tied up a deal.

"You're sure you don't mind focusing on Charlie's room right now?" Vito asked as Charlie ran ahead to examine a heavily chromed motorcycle in front of the Chatterbox. "It's not the project you were planning on, I'm sure."

"It's not, but it's a good change of plans. Having a room or two decorated for kids will only add to the guesthouse's appeal. And that little room off the big one is perfect for that."

"And you're being kind. Charlie's been in a mood, so maybe this will help." They reached Love's Hardware, and Vito held the door for her, then called for Charlie to come join them.

The front of the store was crowded with summer merchandise, garden tools and stacked bags of mulch and grass seed. A faint, pungent smell attested to the fertilizer and weed killer in stock. Farther back, bins of nails and screws and bolts occupied one wall while pipes and sinks and bathtubs dominated the other. Overhead, modern light fixtures, price tags hanging, intermixed with old-fashioned signs advertising long-gone brands of household appliances. The soft sound of R & B played in the background.

A string of small bells chimed on the door as it closed behind them, and the store's owner, Mr. Love, came forward immediately, one weathered brown hand extended, subtly guiding him through the store aisle. His vision wasn't the best, but he still managed his hardware store almost entirely on his own.

"Hey, Mr. Love, it's Lacey. And you remember Vito D'Angelo, right?"

"I sure do, sure do. Glad to see you folks on such a fine day." Mr. Love fumbled for their hands, and then clasped each in a friendly greeting.

"And this is his foster son, Charlie."

"Say hello," Vito prompted the boy, urging him forward.

Charlie scowled as if he might refuse. But as he looked up at Mr. Love, he seemed impressed by the man's age and courtly dignity. "Hi, it's nice to meet you," he said, holding out his hand to shake in a surprising display of good manners.

After Lacey had explained their mission, Mr. Love led them over to the paint section, where Charlie's momentary sweetness vanished. "I want this blue," he said, selecting a bold cobalt paint chip and holding it out as if the decision was made.

Lacey bit her lip. She'd told Charlie he could help pick out the color, but she and her future guests were the ones who'd have to live with it. "How about something a little lighter, Charlie? It's an old-fashioned house, and this is a pretty modern color." She offered up a sample card featuring various shades of blue. "I was thinking of something in this range."

"That's boring. I want this one."

"It's Lacey's decision, buddy," Vito said, putting a firm hand on Charlie's shoulder. "We're guests in her house, and she's nice to let you choose the color blue."

Charlie's lower lip stuck out a mile.

"Let's look at the cobalt in shades," Lacey suggested. "We could have that color, just a little lighter. Do you like this one?" She pointed at a shade halfway down the sample card.

"That one's okay." Charlie pointed at one toward the end, almost as bright as his original pick.

"Charlie. Lacey has the last word."

Lacey bent to see Charlie's downcast face. "I promise I'll take your ideas into consideration."

"Fine." Charlie gave Lacey a dirty look.

"Come on, let's go see the power tools," Vito suggested. "Guy stuff," he added, winking at Lacey.

Immediately, her distress about Charlie's attitude faded as her heart gave a funny little twist.

"I have to let my granddaughter mix the paint or she gets mad at me," Mr. Love said to Lacey. In a lower voice, he added, "I can't see the colors too well, but if you'd like, I can ask her to add in a little more white to whatever shade the boy picked."

"That would be fantastic," Lacey said gratefully. "Thank you."

"Don't you worry about young Charlie," Mr. Love said, patting her arm. "Kids usually come around."

That was true, and besides, Charlie wasn't her problem to worry about. But there was no point in explaining that to Mr. Love, so she let it go.

On the way home, they walked by a group of slightly older boys playing basketball in the park, and Charlie wanted to join in.

"No, buddy," Vito said. "We're painting today."

"I don't wanna paint! I wanna play outside!"

That made sense to Lacey, but Vito shook

his head. "You can run ahead and play basketball outside the guesthouse for a while."

"That's no fun, playing by myself." But Charlie took off ahead of them, staying in sight, but kicking stones in an obvious display of bad temper.

Vito blew out a sigh. "Sure wish there was a manual on how to parent," he said.

"I think you're doing great," she said, reassuring him. "What's Charlie's background, anyway? Was it difficult?"

Vito looked away, then back at her. "Yeah. His mom's an addict. She loves him, but not as much as she loves to get high."

Poor Charlie. "What about his dad?"

Vito looked away again and didn't answer.

A sudden, surprising thought came into Lacey's head: was Charlie *Vito's* biological son?

But no. If Vito had fathered a child, he wouldn't deny it and pretend to just be the foster dad.

"His dad's passed," Vito said finally. "And Mom keeps getting involved with men who rough her up. It happened to Charlie a few times, too, which is why he originally went into foster care. His mom wasn't able to make a change, so Charlie's free for adoption. I hope we'll have that finalized within a few months."

"That's great, Vito." Even as she said it, she wondered how and why he'd gotten involved in foster care. It was so good of him, but not something most single men in their early thirties would consider. "Why did—"

"Charlie learned a rough style of play in some of his old neighborhoods," Vito interrupted quickly, almost as if he wanted to avoid her questions. "And he doesn't have the best social skills. If he's going to play basketball in the park, I need to be there to supervise."

"You could stay with him now. You don't have to help me paint his room."

"Thanks, but no. It's only right that we help. And besides," he said, flashing her a smile, "it's what I want to do."

So they spent the afternoon painting as

a team. Sun poured through the open windows, and birds sang outside. Stroking the brush, and then the roller, across the walls, soothed Lacey's heart. Again, more strongly this time, she got that weird feeling of being a family with Vito.

He was good around the house. He could fix things, he could paint, he could cook. And he liked to do those things with her.

Unlike Gerry, who'd always begged off family chores.

Charlie burst into the room, planted his feet wide and crossed his arms. He looked around the half-painted room, his lip curling. "That's not the color I wanted."

Something about his stance and his expression looked oddly familiar to Lacey, but she couldn't put her finger on what it was.

"The second coat'll make it brighter, buddy," Vito said. "Why don't you stay in here and I'll teach you to paint with the roller?"

"No way. That's boring." Charlie turned to stomp out and landed a foot directly in the tray of paint. When he saw what he'd done, he ran out of the room, tracking paint the whole way.

Vito leaped up and hurried after him, while Lacey raced to wipe up the paint before it dried on the hardwood floors, chuckling a little to herself. With Vito and Charlie around, there would never be a dull moment.

"Oh, man, I'm sorry," Vito said as he returned to see her scrubbing at a last footprint. "Charlie's in time-out in the kitchen, since I can't exactly send him to his room, and he'll be back up in a few minutes to help. Neatly. To make up for this mess."

"It's okay. It's part of having a kid."

Vito sighed. "I guess it is, but I wasn't ready for it. I never know if I'm doing the right thing or not."

"You're doing a good job. Really good." She smiled up at him.

"Thanks. I don't feel so sure."

Just like the other night, their eyes caught and held for a beat too long.

Charlie burst into the room in sock feet

and stood, hands on hips. "I'm here, but I ain't apologizing and I ain't helping." He lifted his chin and glared at Vito as if daring him to exert his authority as a father.

Vito opened his mouth to speak, but Lacey's heart went out to the hurting little boy, and she held up a hand. "Let me talk to him," she said, and walked over to Charlie. "It's been a rough day, hasn't it? But that paint came right off and it won't be a problem."

"So?"

In every stiff line of his body she read a need for a mother's comfort. "Hey," she said, putting an arm around him, "I'm glad you're here and I think this is going to be a great room for you. You can help decorate it."

For a second Charlie relaxed against her, but then he went stiff again and stepped away, his face red. "That's what you said about the paint, and then I got this baby color!" He waved a hand at the nearest wall.

"Oh, honey—"

"Don't call me that! Only my real mom can call me that!"

"Charlie…" Vito said in a warning voice, approaching the two of them.

"She doesn't have any kids! She's not a mom, so why is she acting like one?"

The words rang in Lacey's ears.

It was true. She wasn't a mom, and Charlie, with a child's insight, had seen right into the dream inside her head. On some barely conscious level she'd been pretending that Charlie was her child and Vito was her husband, and it had to stop.

Slowly, she backed away from Charlie just as Vito reached him.

"I want you to apologize to Miss Lacey," Vito said firmly.

"I'm not apologizing!" Tears ran down Charlie's reddened face, but he ignored them, frowning fiercely and thrusting his chest out.

"Charlie." Vito put a hand on the boy's shoulder.

"Don't you touch me! You're not my real dad. And you're ugly, too!" Charlie ran from the room.

Vito's hand went to his scarred face for just a moment, and then he followed Charlie.

Even in the middle of her own hurt feelings, Lacey wanted to comfort him, to tell him he *wasn't* ugly.

But that was exactly the problem. She wasn't the mom of the family. She wasn't the wife.

She never would play that role, and she needed to stop pretending and accept the truth.

Chapter Six

"Let's see if we can scare up a basketball game at the park," Vito said to Charlie the next day after lunch.

"Yeah!" Charlie dropped his handheld game and jumped up.

Vito laughed. He was still getting used to the time frame of an eight-year-old. "In ten minutes, okay? I have to clean up our dishes and make a phone call."

Vito had planned to spend Saturday setting up Charlie's room and looking for jobs online. But Charlie's behavior the previous day had changed his mind. Vito was no expert, but it seemed to him that Charlie needed structure, and chores, and attention. So they'd spent the morning weeding the gardens around the guesthouse, and with a little prodding Charlie had worked hard. He'd even taken a glass of lemonade to Lacey, who was sanding woodwork in the breakfast room, and Vito had heard her talk cheerfully to Charlie, which was a relief. Apparently, she wasn't holding a grudge against Charlie for yesterday's behavior.

So, amends made, Vito and Charlie half walked, half jogged to the park together, bouncing a basketball. Lawn mowers and weed eaters roared, filling the air with the pungent fragrance of vegetation, and several people called greetings from flower beds and front yards. Things weren't much different than when Vito himself had been eight, growing up here.

The call he'd made had been to Troy Hinton, an old acquaintance whose son, Xavier, was just Charlie's age. Troy and Xavier met them by the basketball courts at the park, and immediately, the boys ran out onto the blacktop to play. Vito and Troy sat down on a bench to watch.

Xavier played well for an eight-year-old, making a few baskets, dribbling without too much traveling. Charlie, though, was on fire, making well more than half of the shots he took. Paternal pride warmed Vito's chest. He'd make sure Charlie tried out for the school team as soon as he got to sixth grade.

"That's a good thing you're doing, fostering him," Troy said, nodding toward Charlie. "He seems like he's settling in fine."

That reminded Vito of yesterday, and he shook his head. "A few bumps in the road."

"Yeah?" Troy bent down to flick a piece of dirt off his leg.

"I think he misses his mom. He sees her once a week, but that's hard on a kid."

"Any chance of her getting him back?"

Vito shook his head. "No. Supervised visits is all."

"Gotcha." Troy was watching the two boys play.

Even at eight, Charlie used his elbows and threw a few too many shoves.

"Charlie!" Vito called.

When Charlie looked over, Vito just shook his head. Charlie's mouth twisted, and then he nodded.

"We talked about sportsmanship this morning. I don't know why he thinks he can play street ball here, in the park."

Troy chuckled. "It's a process. And Xavier's holding his own." Indeed, the boy did some fancy footwork and stole the ball from Charlie.

Which was impressive, considering Xavier's background. "How's his health?"

"Almost two years cancer-free."

"That's great." Although Vito had been overseas, he'd heard from Nonna about the careworn single mom who'd come to town to work at Troy's dog rescue, bringing her son who was struggling with leukemia. Now Troy and Angelica were married, with another child, and it was great to know that Xavier was healthy and strong.

"He's doing so well that we can't keep up with him in the summer. So we've got him in a weekday program here at the park. Six hours a day, lots of activity. Charlie should join."

"Well…" Vito thought about it. "That's tempting, but Charlie has a few issues."

"People who run it are good with issues. And you should also bring him to the Kennel Kids." Troy explained the program for at-risk boys, helping once a week at the dog rescue farm Troy operated.

Vito had to thank God for how things were working out here in Rescue River. It was a great place to raise kids. "Sounds perfect, if you've got a space for him."

"Might have one for you, too. I could use a little help."

"Oh, so that's how it is," Vito joked, but truthfully, he was glad to be asked. Vito liked dogs, and Troy. And most of all, he wanted to do positive things for Charlie, and with him. "Sure thing. I can help out."

The boys came running over, panting, and grabbed water bottles to chug.

"You guys should come play!" Charlie said, looking from Vito to Troy.

"Aw, Dad's too tired." Xavier bounced the basketball hard so it went back up higher than his head.

"Who says?" Troy got to his feet and grinned at Vito. "Hintons against D'Angelos, what do you say?"

"I'm not a D'Angelo," Charlie protested.

"But you're going to be, pretty soon." Vito stood, too, and ruffled Charlie's hair. "Meanwhile, let's show these Hintons how it's done."

After an hour of play that left them all breathless and sweating, Troy and Xavier invited Charlie to come out to the farm for a few hours, and Vito agreed. It was good for Charlie to make friends.

But that left Vito with a hole in his day. He'd finished the preliminary work for his online courses, and the term didn't start for another week. Nonna was spending the day visiting at the Senior Towers.

He thought of Troy Hinton, married, raising two kids, the town veterinarian and dog rescue owner, volunteering with the Kennel Kids. What was Vito contributing by comparison? And Troy had a big property to handle, a place for kids to run, while Vito was living in two rooms.

He walked through the park, feeling uncharacteristically blue. There was a soccer game going on, a coed team of kids a little younger than Charlie, and Vito stopped to watch. The game wasn't too serious. Parents chatted with each other in the bleachers while coaches hollered instructions, mostly encouraging rather than overly competitive. Nearby, a family with a new baby sat on a blanket, cheering on their kids who were playing while cuddling with toddlers who looked like twins.

Vito wanted that. Wanted a family, a large family. It was in his blood.

Suddenly, someone tapped his shoulder,

and he turned to see Lacey and another woman, pretty, dark-haired, with Asian features.

"Hi!" the dark-haired woman said, holding out a hand. "I'm Susan Hinton. I've heard a lot about you."

What did that mean? He shook Susan's hand and shot a glance at Lacey. Her cheeks were pink. What had she been telling Susan?

"Vito D'Angelo," he supplied, since Lacey seemed to be tongue-tied. "It's a pleasure. Are you related to Troy?"

"Sure am. I'm married to his brother, Sam."

"I know Sam. Sorry to have missed the wedding." He'd been invited, but he'd been in the thick of his surgery at that point.

"Mindy could score," Lacey said, gesturing toward the soccer game. She looked like a teenager, dressed in cutoffs and a soft blue T-shirt. Her short blond hair lifted and tossed in the breeze, and Vito liked that she didn't glue it down with hair spray.

He felt an urge to brush back a strand that had fallen into her eyes, but that would be completely inappropriate. They weren't that kind of friends.

"C'mon, Mindy, go for it!" Susan yelled, and the little girl in question kicked the ball hard, making a goal. "Good job!"

"Susan's a teacher," Lacey said when the hubbub had died down. "She might have some good ideas about your career change."

"You're switching over to teaching?" Susan asked. "What age of kids?"

"I like the little ones," Vito admitted. "Seems like elementary teachers make a big difference."

"And we need more men in the profession," Susan said promptly. "Are you planning to stay local?"

"If I can find work."

Susan opened her mouth as if she were going to ask another question, but a shout interrupted her. Mindy, the child who'd scored a goal, ran over, accompanied by two little girls about the same age. "Did you see, Mama, did you see?"

"I saw." Susan hugged the little girl close. "You're getting better every day."

Vito was watching the pair, so it took a minute for him to become aware that the other two girls were staring up at him.

"What happened to the side of your face?" one of them asked.

"He looks *mean*," said the other little girl.

The remarks shouldn't have stung—he'd known that was how kids would feel, hadn't he?—but they did, anyway.

"Cheyenne! Shelby!" Susan spun and squatted right in front of the other two girls. "You know it's not polite to make personal remarks about someone's appearance."

"I'm sorry, Miss Hayashi," one of them said right away.

"It's Mrs. Hinton, dummy," the other said. "Don't you know she got married?"

Susan put a hand on each girl's shoulder. "First of all, it's more important to be… Do you remember what?"

"More important to be polite than right," the two and little Mindy chorused.

"And furthermore, Shelby," Susan said sternly, "this gentleman got those injuries serving our country, and you *will* show him the respect he deserves."

Vito didn't know which felt worse: being told how bad he looked by a second-grade-ish little girl, or being defended by a woman approximately half his size. "Hey, it's okay," he said, squatting down, too, making sure his better half was turned toward the girls. "It can be a surprise to see somebody who looks different."

Mindy shoved in front of him. "I'm *glad* he looks different. Different is cool." She reached up and unhooked something from her back and then started fumbling with her arm.

"Don't take it off! Don't take it off!" the other two girls screamed, sounding more excited than upset.

At which point Vito realized that Mindy had a prosthetic arm, which she seemed set on removing.

Other kids ran in their direction, no doubt

attracted by the screams. Vito stood and glanced at Lacey, who gave him a palms up that clearly said she had no idea how to handle the situation.

"Mindy!" Susan's voice was stern, all teacher. "Don't you dare take off that arm. You know the rules."

Mindy's forehead wrinkled, and she and Susan glared at each other. Then, slowly, Mindy twisted something back into place and let go of her prosthetic. "I just wanted to show them that everybody's different, and that's okay," she said sulkily.

Susan knelt and hugged her. "That was a very kind impulse. Now, why don't you girls get back on the field? I think the second half is starting."

Vito took a step back. "Hey, it was nice meeting you," he said to Susan.

"Vito—" Lacey sounded worried.

"Got to go. See you later." What he really needed to do was to be alone. Today's little scene had hammered the truth home to him: he couldn't work with kids in person.

His appearance would create a ruckus that would interfere with their learning.

The trouble was he liked kids. And interacting with them through a computer screen just didn't have the same appeal.

Lacey looked from where Susan was ushering the little girls back into the soccer game, toward the path where Vito was walking away, shoulders slumped.

"I'm headed home," she called to Susan, and then took off after Vito. She couldn't stand what she'd just seen.

He was walking fast enough that she was out of breath by the time she got within earshot. "Vito, wait!"

He turned around to wait for her.

"Where are you going? Are you okay?" she asked breathlessly.

"I'm going for a walk, and I'm fine." His words were uncharacteristically clipped.

"Mind if I come?" She started walking beside him, sure of her welcome. After all, this was Vito. He was always glad to see her.

"Actually…" He walked slowly, glanced over at her. "Look, I'm not fit company. Go on back and hang out with Susan."

She gave him a mock glare. "No way! You hung out with me plenty when I wasn't fit company. I'm just returning the favor to an old friend."

He started to say something, then closed his mouth, and mortification sent heat up Lacey's neck. She was being intrusive. It was one of her flaws, according to Gerry, and she half expected Vito to bite her head off.

But he didn't speak and his face wasn't angry. They walked quietly for a few minutes, past the high school. The fragrance of new-mown grass tickled Lacey's nose. From somewhere, she smelled meat grilling, a summer barbecue.

"Where are you headed?" she repeated, because he hadn't answered. "Can I tag along?" Then she worried she'd pushed too far.

"I'm going to the river. To think." He gave her shoulders a quick squeeze. "And sure, you can come. Sorry to be such a bear."

So she followed him down a little path between the grasses and trees and they emerged on the riverbank. As if by agreement, they both stopped, looking at the sunlight glinting off the water, hearing the wind rustle through the weeping willow trees overhead.

"I'm sorry that happened back there," she said. "That must be hard to deal with, especially..." She trailed off.

"Especially what?"

"Especially when you were always so handsome."

He laughed, shaking his head at the same time. "Oh, Lace. My biggest fan."

She had been, too. In fact, as a younger teen, she'd dreamed of a day when she'd be older, with clear skin and actual curves, and Vito would ask her out. A visceral memory flashed into her mind: lying on the floor of her bedroom, feet propped up on a footstool and CD player blasting out a sad love song, which in her fourteen-year-old brain she'd applied to herself and Vito's lost love.

"You were the best looking of all the guys in your class," she said. "Everyone said so."

He didn't deny it, exactly, but he waved a dismissive hand. "A lot of good it did me. I could barely get a date."

That had to be an exaggeration; she remembered plenty of girls noticing him. But it was true, he hadn't dated as much as you'd expect of a boy with his looks. "You were too nice. You weren't a player."

He laughed. "That's true, I never got that down." They turned and strolled along the river's grassy bank. "Now I look mean, like the little girl said. Maybe I should cultivate a mean persona to match. I'd get all the girls."

"As if that's going to happen." Lacey couldn't imagine Vito being mean. It just wasn't in his nature. "Is that what you want, Vito? All the girls?"

He gave her a look she couldn't read. "Not all. But I'd like to get married, start a family, and I'm not getting any younger."

"Is that why you're adopting Charlie?"

He lifted a shoulder and looked away. "That's part of it."

"As far as getting married," she said, "you could have any woman you wanted."

A muscle contracted in his scarred cheek. "Don't, Lace."

"Don't what?" She stumbled on a root and he automatically caught her arm, steadied her.

"Don't lie to me. If I couldn't get the girls before, I'm not going to get them now."

"I'm not lying. You have a…" She paused, considering how to say it. "You have a rugged appeal."

"Is that so?" He looked over at her, his expression skeptical.

For some reason, her face heated, and she lifted it to cool in the breeze from the river. She focused on the birdcalls and blue sky, visible through a network of green leaves, while she tried to get her bearings.

When she looked back at him, he was still watching her. "Think of Tiffany Townsend," she said, trying to sound offhand. "She was all over you."

He rolled his eyes, just a little, making her remember him as a teen. "Tiffany Townsend isn't what I want."

"What do you want?"

Instead of answering, he walked a few paces to the right and lifted a streamer of honeysuckle growing against a thick strand of trees. Beyond it was a cave-like depression in a natural rock wall. "Wonder if kids are still carving their names in here?"

She laughed. "Lover's Cave. I'd forgotten about it." She followed him inside, the temperature dropping a good few degrees, making a chill rise up on her arms.

Vito pinched off a vine of honeysuckle flowers, inhaled their scent, and then tucked them into Lacey's hair. "For a lovely lady."

Wow. Why wasn't Vito married by now?

He was chivalrous, a natural romantic. Who *wouldn't* want to be with a man like that?

Inside the small enclosure, she turned to him, then stepped back, feeling overwhelmed by the closeness. *Make conversation; this is awkward.* "Did you ever kiss a girl in here?"

He laughed outright. "My *nonna* taught me better than to kiss and tell. Why? Were you kissed in here?"

"No." She remembered bringing Gerry down to the river, showing him the sights of her younger days. She'd hoped to finally get a kiss in Lover's Cave, but he hadn't wanted to follow her inside. Romantic gestures weren't his thing, but that was okay. He'd loved her; she was sure of that.

"What was wrong with the boys in your grade? Why didn't you get kissed here?"

"Guys didn't like my type." She turned away, catching a whiff of honeysuckle.

He touched her face, making her look at him. "What type is that?"

"Shy. Backward."

"Are you still?"

Lacey's heart was pounding. "I... I might be."

His fingers still rested on her cheek, featherlight. "Don't be nervous. It's just me."

A hysterical giggle bubbled up inside her, along with a warm, melty breathlessness. She couldn't look away from him.

He cupped her face with both hands. Oh, wow, was he really going to kiss her? Her heart was about to fly out of her chest and she blurted out the first nervous thought she had. "You never answered my question."

"What was it? I'm getting distracted." He smiled a little, but his eyes were intense, serious.

He was *incredibly* attractive, scars and all.

"I asked you," she said breathlessly, "what *do* you want, if you don't want someone like Tiffany?"

"I want..." He paused, looked out through the veil of honeysuckle vines and let his hands fall away from her face. Breathed in, breathed out, audibly, and then eased out of the cave, holding the honeysuckle curtain for her, but careful not to touch her. "I want what I can't have."

Suddenly chilled, Lacey rubbed her bare arms, looking away from him. Whatever Vito wanted, it was obviously not her.

Chapter Seven

"Come on, Nonna, let's go sit on the porch." Vito was walking his grandmother out of the kitchen after dinner. Nonna hadn't eaten much of it despite his and Charlie's cajoling. Vito wished Lacey had stayed to eat with them, but she'd had something else urgent to do.

Most likely, urgently avoiding *him*. And rightly so. He was avoiding her, too, and kicking himself for that little romantic interlude in Lover's Cave.

"I'm a little tired for the porch, dear." Nonna held tightly on to his arm.

She sounded depressed, something Lacey

had mentioned was common in patients recovering from a heart attack. Activity and socializing were part of the solution, so Vito pressed on. "But you've been in your room all day. A talk and a little air will do you good."

"Well…" She paused. "Will you sit with me?"

"Nothing I'd rather do." He kissed her soft cheek, noticing the fragrance of lavender that always clung to her, and his heart tightened with love.

He and Nonna walked slowly down the guesthouse hall. She still clung to his arm, and when they got to the bench beside the door, she stopped. "I'll just…rest here a minute. Could you get me another glass of that iced tea? I'm so thirsty."

"Sure." He settled her on the bench and went back to the kitchen to pour iced tea, looking out into the driveway to see if, by chance, Lacey had come in without his noticing. He'd feel better if she were here. Only because Nonna wasn't feeling well.

When he reached the guesthouse door with the tea, he saw that Nonna was already out on the porch. "Charlie helped me out," she said, gesturing to where the boy was shooting hoops across the street. "He's a good boy."

He set their tea on the table between the rocking chairs and sat down. The evening air was warm, but the humidity was down and the light breeze made for comfortable porch-sitting. In fact, several people were outside down the block, in front of the Senior Towers. A young couple walked by pushing a stroller, talking rapidly in Spanish. Marilyn Smith strolled past the basketball hoop with her Saint Bernard, and Charlie and his friend stopped playing to pet it and ask her excited questions.

Evening in a small town. He loved it here.

"Tell me about your course work, dear," Nonna said. "Is it going well?"

"Just finished a couple of modules today. It's interesting material."

"And you like taking a class on the computer?"

He shrugged. "Honestly, I'd rather be in a classroom where I could talk and listen, but we don't have a college here, and this is the easiest, cheapest option."

"That's just what Lou Ann Miller says. She's almost done with her degree. At her age!"

They chatted on about Vito's courses and Lou Ann and other people they knew in common, greeted a few neighbors walking by.

After a while, Vito noticed that Nonna had gotten quiet, and he looked over to see her eyes blinking closed. In the slanting evening sunlight, her skin looked wrinkled like thin cloth, and her coloring wasn't as robust as he'd have liked to see.

Lacey's little car drove into the driveway. She pulled behind the guesthouse, and moments later the back screen door slammed.

Normally, she'd have come in by the front porch, stopping to pull a couple of weeds from the flower bed and say hello to Nonna. So she was still avoiding him, obviously, but at least she was home in case Nonna needed her.

Nonna started awake and looked around as if she was confused. "Tell me about your courses, dear," she said.

"We just talked about that." Vito studied her. "Are you feeling okay? Do you want to go inside?"

"I'm fine. I meant your job hunt. Tell me about your job hunt." She smiled reassuringly, looking like her old self.

"I keep seeing jobs that look interesting, but they're all in person." He paused, then added, "I want an online job."

As usual, Nonna read his mind. "You can't hide forever," she said, patting his hand.

"You're right, and I'm a coward for wanting to hide behind the computer. Except...would you want your kids to have a scary teacher?"

"I'd want them to have a smart, caring

teacher. And besides, once people get to know you, they forget about those little scars. I have."

It was what Lacey had said, too. It was what Troy had said. It was even what his friends in the VA support group said. He didn't know why he was having such a hard time getting over his scarred face.

And okay, he was bummed for a number of reasons. If things had been different, if Charlie hadn't needed a home and if he hadn't been so scarred, then maybe he and Lacey could have made a go of things. She'd seemed a little interested, for a minute there.

But things weren't different, and he needed to focus on the here and now, and on those who needed him. He glanced over at Nonna.

She was slumped over in her chair at an odd angle, her eyes closed.

"Nonna!" He leaped up and tried a gentle shake of her shoulders that failed to wake her. "Charlie, come here!" he called over his shoulder.

He lifted his grandmother from the chair

and carried her to the door just as Charlie arrived and opened it for him. "Is she okay?" Charlie asked.

"Not yet. Get Lacey, now!" Vito carried Nonna into her bedroom and set her gently on the bed. He should never have encouraged her to go out on the porch. On the other hand, what if she'd fainted in her room, alone? What had brought this on? Up until tonight she'd seemed to be improving daily.

Lacey burst into the room, stethoscope in hand, and bent over the bed, studying Nonna. "What happened?"

"She wasn't feeling well, and then she passed out."

Lacey took her pulse and listened. "It's rapid but…" She stopped, listened again. "It's settling a bit." She opened Nonna's bedside drawer and pulled out a pen-like device, a test strip, and some kind of a meter. "I'm going to test her blood sugar."

Charlie hovered in the door of the room as Lacey pricked Nonna's finger, and Vito debated sending him away. But he and Nonna were developing a nice friendship, and Charlie deserved to be included in what was going on.

Nonna's eyes fluttered open. She was breathing fast, like she'd run a race.

Vito's throat constricted, looking at her. She was fragile. Why hadn't he realized how fragile she was?

Lacey frowned at the test strip, left the room and returned with a hypodermic needle. "Little pinch," she said to Nonna as she extracted clear liquid from a small bottle and injected her arm. "Your blood sugar is through the roof. What happened? It hasn't been this high in weeks!"

There was a snuffling sound from the doorway; Charlie was crying. Vito held out an arm, and Charlie ran and pressed beside him, looking at Nonna with open worry.

Lacey propped Nonna up and sat on the bed, holding her hand. "Are you feeling better? You passed out."

"Was it the cake?" Charlie blurted out.

Vito's head spun to look at the boy at the

same time Lacey's did. "What cake?" they asked in unison.

Charlie pressed his lips together and looked at Nonna, whose expression was guilty.

"I… I gave him money…" Nonna broke off and leaned back against the pillow, her eyes closing.

"What happened?" Vito set Charlie in front of him, put his hands on the boy's shoulders and studied him sternly. "Tell the truth."

"She gave me money and asked me to get her cake from the bakery. I didn't know what to do! I wanted her to have a treat. She said it would be our secret. And she gave me the rest of the money so I could get something, too." Charlie was crying openly now. "I'm sorry! I didn't know it would hurt her.'"

Vito shook his head and patted the boy's shoulder, not sure whether to comfort or punish him. "Remember, you're supposed to come ask me, not just go do something another adult tells you to do. Even if it's Nonna."

"Is she going to be okay?"

"She'll be okay." Lacey gave Charlie's hand a quick squeeze. "But your dad's right. Don't ever bring her something to eat again without asking one of us."

Even in the midst of his worries, Vito noticed that Lacey had automatically called him Charlie's dad. He liked the sound of that.

But he was second-guessing himself for bringing Charlie to live here at all. The kid was eight. He didn't know how to properly assist in the care of a very sick elderly woman, and he didn't have an idea of consequences.

Nonna said something, her voice weak, and Lacey put a hand on Charlie's arm. "Let's listen to Nonna."

"I...told him...to do it. Not his fault." She offered up a guilty smile that was a shadow of her usual bright one.

"Nonna! This is serious. We're going to have to take you to the emergency room to get you checked out."

"Oh, no," Nonna said as Charlie broke into fresh tears. "I just want to rest."

Lacey bit her lip and looked at Vito. "I might be able to talk Dr. Griffin into coming over to take a look at her," she said. "It would be exhausting for her to go to the ER, and I *think* she's going to be okay once her sugar comes down, but I'm not qualified to judge."

"If you could do that, I'd be very grateful." He knew that old Dr. Griffin lived right down the street.

"Okay. Charlie, would you like to come help me get the doctor?"

Charlie nodded, sniffling.

"Could you run upstairs and get my purse out of my bedroom?"

"Sure!" Charlie ran.

Vito was grateful. Lacey had every reason to be angry at the boy, but she was instead helping him to feel better by giving him a job. But that was how she was: forgiving, mature, wise beyond her years.

"Doc owes me a favor," Lacey said quietly

to Vito. "I'm sure he'll come, if he's home. Just sit with her until we get back. It'll only be five minutes."

He nodded, gently stroking Nonna's arm, and Lacey and Charlie went out the door.

Beside Nonna's bed was a photo of him and his brother as children. She'd taken them in and raised them after their parents' accident, putting aside her bridge games and bus trips to rejoin the world of PTA meetings and kids' sporting events. And she'd done it with such good cheer that he'd never, until recently, understood the burden it must have been to her.

Now it was time for him to return the favor. To make sure that she was getting the very best care she could.

Which meant that later tonight if, God willing, Nonna was okay, Vito needed to have a very serious talk with Lacey.

After ushering Doc Griffin out the door with profuse thanks, Lacey walked back into the guesthouse as Vito emerged from

Nonna's room, gently closing her door behind him.

"She's already asleep," he said. "She's exhausted, but she said to tell you again that she's sorry."

Lacey shook her head and paced the hall. "I'm the one who should be sorry. I should have been keeping closer track of her food."

"She's an adult," Vito said. "She made a choice." But something in his voice told her he didn't completely believe what he was saying, and what he said next confirmed it. "If you have a minute, could we talk?"

"Of course." She gestured for him to come into the front sitting room as her heart sank.

She'd been avoiding him hard all week, since that crazy moment in Lover's Cave. She'd thought he was going to kiss her, and she was sure that expectation had shone on her face. But instead of doing it, he'd gently pushed her away from him.

He was too kind to give her a real rejection, but even his careful one had made her feel like a loser.

He stood in the middle of the room, looking more masculine than ever amidst the delicate Victorian furnishings, and she realized he was waiting for her to sit down first. Who had those kind of manners these days?

Vito, that was who. And she was starting to care for him more than she should. Even though he didn't return the feelings, and nothing would come of it, she felt guilty. What would Gerry think if he knew that she was looking at his best friend in a way she'd once reserved for him?

Or, if the truth be told, in a different way but with the same end game? Because there weren't two men in the world more different than Vito and Gerry. And while Gerry's confidence and swagger had swept her away when she was young, Vito's warm and caring style appealed to her now.

He was still standing, waiting, so she sank down onto the chesterfield and pulled her feet up under her, leaving Vito to take the matching chair. It was a little small for him. Good. Maybe this conversation would be brief.

He cleared his throat. "I was wondering if you've been avoiding me."

Lacey felt her eyebrows shoot up, and against her will, heat rose into her cheeks. "Avoiding you?"

He nodded patiently. "After what happened last weekend. You know, at Lover's Cave."

She blew out a breath. She'd hoped to avoid that topic, but here he was bringing it out into the open to deal with. "I, um…" She wanted to lie, but couldn't bring herself to do it. "Maybe a little," she admitted.

"I thought so." He leaned forward, elbows on knees, and held her gaze. "You don't have to worry about a repeat. And you don't have to stay away from your own house to keep me at bay."

Keep *him* at bay? But of course, chivalrous to the core, Vito would put it like that. Make it seem like she was the one rejecting him, when in point of fact, it had been the other way around.

She swallowed and tore her eyes away from his. And for the life of her, she couldn't think of what to say.

How could she respond when she didn't even know what she felt, herself? When these feelings about Vito tugged at her loyalty to Gerry, even making her question some of her husband's behaviors? When Vito didn't seem to share her attraction at all?

"The thing is," he said, "I'm worried about Nonna's care. If Charlie and I are keeping you from focusing on that, then we should move out."

"She wouldn't like that."

"But if you hadn't come home tonight, and known just what to do, and given her that injection, something much worse could have happened, right?"

Miserably, Lacey twisted her hands together, staring at the floor. "I'm really sorry. I can see why you think I've been neglectful."

"That's not it. I don't think you and she ever had an arrangement where you had to be here with her 24/7. Did you?"

"No." Honesty compelled her to add, "But part of the appeal of living here was that she'd have me around a lot while I remodeled. Which I usually am. It's just been a week of running errands instead of remodeling."

He nodded. "I've been too focused on my own stuff, too, and apparently, it's given Nonna and Charlie too much time to get into trouble together."

"Does Charlie understand that he's not to do that anymore?"

"Yes. He was pretty upset when he saw Nonna passed out. He's grown very fond of her." He looked into her eyes again. "And of you. You've been very kind to him."

"He's a good kid."

He nodded. "So, this arrangement is working out well for Nonna, and well for Charlie. It's just you and me who need to manage our...interactions."

If he could be up front and honest, so could she. "I won't need to avoid you if you're serious about no repeat of that. I... I'm not over Gerry, you see." She fingered the necklace where she wore his wedding ring. "I know it's been over a year, which some people say is enough time, but it's not. He was everything to me."

A shadow crossed Vito's face, and for the first time she realized that he didn't talk much about Gerry. She wondered why. They'd been close comrades, right? Close enough for Gerry to come home with Vito on leave from the army. "You know what he was like," she persisted. "What a great guy he was."

Vito nodded once. "I know what he was like."

"So you can see why...well, why it's hard to get over him. He'll always be my hero."

A muscle worked in Vito's scarred face. "I understand. And believe me, the last thing I want is to displace that feeling in you. So please, stay and care for Nonna and don't worry about Charlie and me."

He stood and walked quickly out of the room.

And Lacey stared after him, wondering why it seemed that he was leaving a lot unsaid.

Chapter Eight

Vito was deep into finishing a research paper on the educator John Dewey when Charlie barged into his room. "Nonna's bored," he announced.

"Bored?" Vito came slowly back to twenty-first-century Ohio. "You're bored?"

"Well, yeah," Charlie said thoughtfully, "a little. But I came to tell you that *Nonna* is bored."

That brought Vito to full attention. "Did she ask you to get her sweets again?"

"No." Charlie shook his head vigorously. "She wouldn't. But she wants me to play a card game called Briscola, and it's too hard.

And she wants me to watch TV with her, only I don't like her shows."

"I'll go spend some time with her." Vito ruffled Charlie's hair. "You probably want to go outside and ride that bike, don't you?" He'd fixed up an old one for Charlie over the weekend.

"Yeah," Charlie said, looking relieved that Vito understood. "Can I?"

"Let's see who's outside. If you stay on this block and be careful of cars, it's okay."

After he'd walked out with Charlie and made sure there were several parents in yards up and down the street, keeping an eye on the kids, Vito went back inside and headed toward Nonna's room. He'd stayed up late working on his research paper and spent most of the day on it, as well, and he felt like the letters on the computer monitor were still bouncing in front of his eyes. But it was all good. He was finding all the teaching theories extraordinarily interesting and it made him certain he'd done the right thing, enrolling in school.

Distracted, he tapped on the edge of Nonna's open door and walked in before realizing that Lacey was there, sitting beside Nonna, both of them engrossed in a television show.

A week had passed since Nonna's health scare and their talk, and they were settling into a routine in which Lacey spent more time at home. A routine that most emphatically did *not* include strolls to Lover's Cave. In fact, it barely included being in the same room together.

Lacey glanced up, saw him and looked away.

Nonna clicked off the television. "I can't believe he picked the blonde. I'm very disappointed in that young man."

"Well, she *was* the prettiest," Lacey said, laughing. "But you're right. I don't see the relationship lasting very long."

"Hey, Nonna." Vito bent over to kiss his grandmother's cheek, conscious that it was the first time he'd seen her that day. He'd been neglectful, working on this paper. He'd do better tomorrow.

The silver lining was that Lacey was spending more time with Nonna, staying home more. He'd heard her up at all hours, working on the renovations. Now, he realized guiltily that one reason she might be staying up late was that Nonna was needing her companionship during the day. Which was partly her job, but also partly his responsibility.

Lacey stood up. "I should go get some stuff done." It was clearly an excuse to get away from Vito.

Perversely, that made him want her to stay.

Apparently, Nonna felt the same. "Could you wait just a minute, dear? There's something I want to talk to you two about."

"O-kaaay." She sat down again with obvious reluctance.

Vito focused on his grandmother. "Charlie says you're bored, Nonna."

"Oh, my, bored doesn't begin to describe it." She patted Lacey's hand. "Although it's not for this one's lack of trying."

"I can't hang out as much as I'd like,"

Lacey said apologetically. "I've got to finish the renovations before the end of the summer, and there's so much to do. But I was thinking, maybe you're well enough to do more of the activities over at the Senior Towers."

"That's a great idea," Vito said, relieved. "Don't they have a bridge group?"

"Yes, and a drop-in lunch program, as well." Lacey smiled at Nonna. "You'd definitely get more exciting lunch choices over there than you get when I fix lunch. And it would get you walking more, which would be great for your health."

"How does that sound, Nonna?"

She shrugged. "Good, I guess," she said. "But..." She trailed off, plucking at the edge of her blanket.

"But what?"

She looked up. "I need a project."

"Like what, a craft project?"

"No, I want to start something new. With people."

That made sense; Nonna wasn't a sit-home-and-knit type of person, or at least, she hadn't been. "Like when you started your baking club that burned everything? Or that barbershop quartet, back when we were kids?" Vito smiled, remembering the off-key singing that had emanated from the big old house's front room when the ladies came to practice. Both groups had been disasters, but entertaining for all involved. Everyone wanted to join in Nonna's projects because she was so much fun as a person.

It made all the sense in the world that she would want to do something like that again.

"Do you have any ideas of what you might want to do?" Lacey asked her.

"Well…" She smiled winningly.

Vito shook his head. "Nonna, when you get that look on your face, I get very afraid."

"What's the idea?" Lacey sounded amused.

Nonna pushed herself up, looking livelier than she'd been the past week. "All right, I'll tell you. You know the show we were just watching?"

"*Bachelor Matches*, sure," Lacey said.

"But what's that got to do with you having a project?"

Nonna clasped her hands together and swung her legs to the side of her bed. "I want to start a new matchmaker service in Rescue River."

"What?" Vito's jaw about dropped. "Why?"

"I don't think—" Lacey began.

"You remember the stories from the old country," Nonna interrupted, gripping Vito's hand. "My Tia Bianca, she was a *paraninfo*. Known for matchmaking throughout our village and beyond. She continued until she died at ninety-seven, and the whole region came to her funeral."

Vito nodded, frowning. He did remember the stories, but he wondered what was behind this.

"I need to start with some test clients," she continued, "and because of all you two have done for me, you can have the honor. For free!"

"Oh, Nonna, no," Lacey said. "I don't

think this is a good idea. I don't want you to overexert yourself."

"She's right." Vito moved to sit beside his grandmother. The last thing he needed was Nonna trying to match him up with some unsuspecting woman who would be horrified by his scars.

"If I don't do this, then what do I have to live for?" Nonna's chin trembled. "Why do I even get up in the morning? Of what use am I to the world?" She buried her face in thin, blue-veined hands, her shoulders shaking.

Vito looked over at Lacey and saw his own concern mirrored on her face.

"Nonna, you have so much to live for!" she said.

"So many people who love you," Vito added, putting an arm around her shoulders.

"But none of it *means* anything!" she said, her face still buried in her hands.

Tears. Vito couldn't handle a woman's tears. "Oh, well, Nonna, if it's that important to you..."

"I could maybe see it if you get someone else involved to help you," Lacey said. "Someone sensible like Lou Ann Miller or Miss Minnie Falcon."

Nonna lifted her head, her teary face transformed by a huge smile. "Yes, they can help, both of them!"

"Good," Lacey said. "And not too much at once. Don't get carried away."

"It'll be just the two of you to start. Now, Vito. What do you want in a woman?"

Vito blinked. How had she recovered from her tears so quickly? Had he missed something?

Or had Nonna been hoodwinking them?

"Could you get me a tablet of paper, dear?" Nonna said to Lacey. "I don't want to miss a word."

"Here you go," Lacey said, handing Nonna a legal pad and a pencil. "And now I've got to get to sanding woodwork."

"Oh, stay, dear. I want to talk to you, too."

Lacey laughed. "Don't you think these interviews should be private?" She spun and walked toward the door.

Vito watched her go, thinking of Nonna's question. The truth was, he wanted someone like Lacey. But because of the secret he had promised to keep, he could never, ever have her.

The next Saturday, Lacey climbed out of her car at A Dog's Last Chance, Troy Hinton's animal rescue farm. As she stretched her arms high, she felt like a weight was gone from her shoulders.

Grasses blew in the soft breeze and looking off to the fenced area by the barn, she could see one dog's shiny black fur, another's mottled brown and white coat. Beside her, the creek rushed, a soothing sound, and red-winged blackbirds perched on the fence.

It was good to get away from the guesthouse. Good to do something for others.

Good to get away from Vito and the constant tension of trying to avoid him.

He'd been in her thoughts so much lately, and in a confusing way. He was so hardworking—up late most nights at his computer, making steady progress toward finishing his degree. He spent time with Charlie every evening, getting involved in the life of the town, even lending a hand with the youth soccer team when one of the coaches had a family emergency.

And he was so patient with Nonna, whose matchmaking service was going full speed ahead, obviously giving the woman something fun to do, but in the process, making Lacey uncomfortable.

A shiny new SUV pulled up beside her car, and Lacey was surprised to see her friend Susan getting out. "Nice car!" she said, remembering the rusty subcompact that Susan had driven when she'd lived for a year at the unrenovated guesthouse.

Susan made a face. "Sam. Just because we're expecting, he thinks we need to have a huge vehicle. I had to talk him down from a full-size van."

"How are you feeling?" Lacey could now ask the question without even a twinge of pain, and that told her she was moving forward, getting over her miscarriage and ready to celebrate other people's happiness.

"I'm feeling great, but Sam treats me like I'm made of glass." Susan rolled her eyes. "He didn't want me to come today. He's afraid one of the big dogs will knock me down. Like I haven't done this eighty thousand times before. And like a stumble would hurt the baby!"

"He loves you."

"He does." Susan's eyes softened. "And he's a control freak. But speaking of men... how's Vito?"

Lacey shrugged. "He's fine. Seems busy."

"You don't see much of him?"

"Well, since he's staying at the guesthouse, of course I see him. But we keep to ourselves."

"By choice, or would you like to see more of him?"

Lacey met her friend's perceptive eyes and looked away. "It's by choice. He makes me nervous."

"Nervous? Why?"

Lacey shrugged. "I don't know. He's so…"

"Big? Manly?"

Lacey laughed and shook her head a little. "Something like that. Come on, you've got to show me the ropes before all the kids arrive."

Susan was a longtime volunteer at the Kennel Kids, and she'd talked Lacey into getting involved. Lacey's therapist thought it was a good idea, too—a way to be involved with others and kids, not necessarily babies but with people. Making a difference.

"Speaking of Vito…" Susan said as they approached the barn where the sound of dogs barking was more audible.

Or at least, that was what Lacey thought her friend had said. "What?" she called over a new wave of barking.

"He's here. Vito." Susan gestured toward the barn, where Vito and Charlie stood talking to Troy Hinton, who ran the place and the Kennel Kids.

Lacey swallowed. What was he doing here?

Just then, he turned around and saw her.

"What are you doing here?" he asked, sounding surprised.

"My question, too." They both looked at each other, and Lacey saw in Vito's eyes the same ambivalence she felt herself.

Susan nudged her. "I'm gonna go get set up. Come over when you're ready. No rush."

"Charlie's doing Kennel Kids," Vito explained.

Relief washed over Lacey, along with something like disappointment. "Oh. So you're just dropping him off?"

"I'm…actually staying to help. Unless that's a problem?"

She lifted her hands, palms out. "No! No, it's fine."

Across the barn, Troy Hinton was hoisting a dog crate to his shoulder. "If anyone has a free hand, we could use your help here," he called.

Lacey moved forward at the same time Vito did, and they jostled each other. And then bounced apart like two rubber balls.

"Sorry!" they both said simultaneously, and Vito stepped back to let her go ahead.

Lacey blushed as she hurried toward Troy. She started to lift a crate.

"Vito, could you help her with that?" Troy nodded her direction. "It's a heavy one."

So she and Vito took ends of the crate and followed Troy.

"Put it down there. We like to have a few crates out here for the dogs to get away from the kids. It's a tough gig for them. Could you two bring one more so I can get started with these kids?"

"Sure." Vito headed back, and then turned to see if she was coming.

She followed reluctantly. Why had she and Vito ended up together? Why wasn't it Susan over here with her?

"Hey, look, why don't you go ahead and help Susan?" Vito said, apparently reading her mind. "I can get that last crate."

"No, it's okay. I'll help you. It's too heavy."

Vito gave her a look. "I'm every bit as

strong as I used to be, even if I do have a few injuries."

"I know that!" Then, ashamed of her exasperated tone, she followed him into the barn and took the bull by the horns. "I'm sorry if this is awkward, Vito. I wish it wasn't."

"You don't want to be around me?"

"It's not that. I just…" More seriously, she was worried he didn't want to be around her.

"Hey, D'Angelo, c'mon! We don't have all day here!" Troy sounded impatient.

Lacey flinched and stole a glance at Vito. That kind of thing had always made Gerry livid; he'd hated to be corrected. It was a guy thing.

Except, to her surprise, Vito laughed. "That's rich, coming from you, Hinton." And then he hustled over to the crate. "Guess we'd better get a move on."

She hurried to help him, wondering as she did what it meant that Vito hadn't gotten angry.

Had Gerry been unusually touchy?

She went to the crate and lifted the other

side, breathing in the good smells—hay and animals. And maybe it was the thought of hay, but her necklace felt itchy on her neck.

"Dad!" Charlie ran over, his whole face lit up in a smile. "Can I get a dog? Mr. Hinton said they need homes." He jogged alongside them as they carried out the large crate.

Vito went still, looking at Charlie, then at Lacey. "It's the first time he called me 'Dad,'" he whispered.

Lacey wanted to hug both of them, but her hands were full, so she settled for a *"Wow"* mouthed across the crate as they continued carrying it out.

"Hey, Lacey," Charlie added, coming up beside her, obviously unaware of the emotions he'd evoked. "Want me to help with that? That's no job for a girl."

Lacey chuckled. "Girls can do a lot of jobs, including moving things. But yes, if you'd like to, you can take that corner." She winked meaningfully at Vito, warning him to slow down.

He gave a subtle nod, and something arced

between them. It was nice to be able to communicate without words sometimes.

After they'd put the crate down, Charlie grinned at her. "*You* wouldn't mind having a dog around, would you, Miss Lacey?"

He was way too cute with that grin. She couldn't resist ruffling his hair. "I won't answer that on the grounds that it might incriminate me with your dad," she said, "but confidentially... I do like dogs."

"See, Dad?"

"Way to throw me under the bus," Vito complained, but there was a smile in his voice.

"Can we get one?"

Vito held up a hand. "That's not a decision we're going to make today."

Charlie looked like he wanted to whine, but shouts from a couple of newly arrived boys distracted him and he ran off. Vito watched him go, shaking his head. "It's hard for me to deny him anything."

A man Lacey knew vaguely emerged from the barn with two pit bulls on leads. As he approached the boys, Charlie took several steps back in obvious fear.

The man clearly noticed. "Hey, Troy," he called, "we have some new Kennel Kids here today. You want to give the bully breeds talk?"

She and Vito drifted over and listened while Troy explained that it was all in how the pit bull was raised, how some were taught to fight while others were raised in a gentle environment, how one always had to be careful in approaching a dog like this.

Troy's words triggered a thought. Charlie had apparently been raised in a rough environment, and he, too, acted out sometimes; he needed to be approached with care. But with love—the kind of love that Vito was so unselfishly offering him—he was starting, even now, to grow into his potential and to become the person God had made him to be.

She watched as one of the smaller pit bulls, a white female named Gracie, was brought out and went from boy to boy. The group started dissolving, some of the boys playing with puppies, others learning to clean kennels, others helping to leash and train dogs. Charlie knelt, and the white pit bull approached him slowly, cautiously.

"Hold out your hand so she can sniff it," Vito encouraged, and after a moment's hesitation, Charlie did.

Watching Vito, she saw someone so much more than the handsome older boy who'd protected her from school bullies when she was younger. He was fatherly now, a man, a hero. He accepted what had happened to him and ran with it, growing into a person of value.

But then again, the seed of the man he'd become had been present in the kind, handsome boy next door.

"Lacey!" Susan gave her a light punch on the shoulder, and she started and turned to her friend. "I've been trying to get your attention forever." She looked where Lacey was looking, and then a slow smile broke out across her face. "Are you *sure* you don't have feelings?"

"No! It's just Vito."

"Somehow, I'm not convinced."

"No way! The truth is, I keep thinking about Gerry."

One of the other volunteers turned. "Gerry McPherson? Boy, that guy was a piece of work."

Lacey cocked her head to one side, feeling her smile slip a little.

"What does *that* mean?" Susan asked, her voice protective.

Lacey looked at the other volunteer, and suddenly, she didn't want to hear what he was going to say.

And then Vito stepped up beside her. "Gerry McPherson was my friend and Lacey's husband." He put an arm around her, a tense arm. "And he died serving our country." His chin lifted a little and he gave the man a level stare.

The other guy raised his hands. "Hey, didn't mean anything." He turned and walked rapidly away.

Susan gave Lacey a curious look and went

over to help one of the younger Kennel Kids, who was having trouble unhooking a black Lab's leash.

"Thanks." Lacey sidestepped away from Vito so she could see him better, and immediately he let his arm drop from her shoulders.

A chill ran over her where his arm had been.

What had the man meant, that Gerry was a piece of work?

She didn't want to face the tiny sliver of doubt that had pierced her.

A couple of hours later, Vito stood up from repairing a broken crate and was startled to find himself surrounded: Susan on one side and Troy's wife, Angelica, on the other.

"So, Vito," Angelica said, "what's going on between you and Lacey?"

"Not one thing. Why?"

"Oh, just wondering." The two women sat down beside him, each working on one of the broken crates.

He wasn't lying about nothing going on, at least not in a guy sense; there wasn't anything of the dating variety going on, that was for sure. On the other hand, there was a lot going on emotionally, every time he saw Lacey.

Man, that had been a close one with that stupid guy almost revealing something bad about Gerry. Lacey had looked so shocked and stricken that he hadn't been able to handle it.

She for sure still believed the best about Gerry. And that was good. He'd always remain a hero in her eyes.

And Gerry *had* definitely had a heroic side. In battle, there wasn't another man in the world Vito would've trusted more. They'd saved each other's skins more than once.

But the home front—specifically, women—had been Gerry's downfall. Something rotten in the way he was raised, or maybe the fact that he'd been so handsome and suave. Too many women had flocked to him, and

Gerry hadn't ever been taught how to treat women with respect. To him, a woman who threw herself at him was fair game.

Any woman was fair game. Lacey definitely hadn't thrown herself at him; she wouldn't have known how. But she'd gotten swept away and before Vito could turn around and warn her, she'd gone and fallen for Gerry.

Vito had tried to talk her out of it, but that had been a miserable failure. Once someone was that far gone, you couldn't bring her back.

At that point, the only thing he could do was to insist that if Gerry wanted Lacey, he needed to marry her, not just use her and throw her away.

It had just about killed him to do it, because by that time, he'd thought Lacey was something pretty special himself. Talking his friend into marrying her was like cutting off his own arm. He'd had to admit, just to himself, that he'd been waiting for Lacey to get old enough that he could honorably ask her out.

Gerry had beaten him to it, had gotten in there and stolen her heart.

And he'd treated her despicably.

And now Vito was in a position of hiding Gerry's wrongdoing from the woman he still, if the truth be told, carried a torch for.

"Earth to Vito," Angelica teased, and he snapped back into the here and now. "You *sure* there's nothing going on?"

"I'm sure," he said heavily. "And there never will be anything going on."

Chapter Nine

The next Friday, Vito heard a high-pitched shout from Nonna's room. "Vito! Lacey!"

He scrambled up from the computer and down the stairs on Lacey's heels. "What's wrong, Nonna?" she was asking as they both entered Nonna's room.

"Are you okay?" he asked his grandmother, who was sitting at the small writing desk looking perfectly fine. In fact, her color was better than he'd ever seen it.

Lacey put a hand on Nonna's shoulder. "You scared us. What's going on?"

"It's my first success," the older woman said. "I found you both dates for tonight!"

Vito had to restrain himself from rolling his eyes. Just what he needed, a blind date.

"Tonight?" Lacey sounded just as distressed as Vito felt. "I... I have plans."

Nonna's eyes sparkled behind her glasses. "The same plans you've had for the past three Friday nights, young lady? A date with a paint can?"

Lacey smiled ruefully. "Actually...yes."

Nonna rubbed her hands together. "I hope you both have some dressy clothes. You'll need to be ready at six o'clock."

Vito groaned inwardly. The last thing he wanted was to put on a suit. "Why dressy? This is Rescue River."

"You both have reservations with your dates at Chez la Ferme."

"No way!" Vito said.

"That's not how you do a blind date, Nonna." Lacey's forehead creased. "For one thing, it's really expensive."

"You get coffee first," Vito added. And then he processed what Lacey had said and looked over at her. How would she know? Was she doing online dating?

He found her looking back at him with a similar question in her eyes, and he felt himself flushing. The truth was, he *had* put his profile up on a Christian dating site a couple of times. And he'd gotten no results worth pursuing, which he attributed to women being turned off by his ugly mug. Or his lack of wealth.

"What if we don't like them, Nonna? Then we're stuck spending hours together." Lacey sank down onto the edge of Nonna's bed, facing them both.

"Whereas with coffee," Vito added, "you can escape after half an hour."

"You're taking a negative attitude," Nonna said. "Why do you think you'll want to escape?"

Vito looked at Lacey, and she looked back at him, and they both laughed. And then he narrowed his eyes at her. So she *had* online dated. But when?

Nonna steepled her hands and stared down

at the floor. "I'm sorry," she said. "Do you want me to cancel the whole thing?" Her tone was desolate.

Vito looked at her bowed head and slumped shoulders and his heart melted. "No, Nonna, it's okay. I'm game. But just this once."

"Me, too," Lacey said with a sigh. "Who's my date?"

Nonna smiled gleefully up at them. "It's a surprise! You won't know until you get to the restaurant."

"Wait," Vito said. "We're *both* at Chez la Ferme tonight? Why there?"

"It's the only nice place in town. I'm so excited for you. You're going to have a wonderful time."

There was no trace of her former sadness, and Vito studied her narrowly. He had the feeling he'd just been manipulated.

"Be ready at six. You're meeting your dates at six thirty."

As they walked out, Vito couldn't help shaking his head. That Nonna. She really was a matchmaker, and she was also someone to whom he, at least, couldn't say no.

At five minutes before six, Vito came out of his room at the guesthouse. He'd driven Charlie over to a new friend's house, and as a result, he'd had to get ready quickly. Not that it mattered. Less time to spend in this necktie that felt like it was strangling him.

He needed to work on his attitude, he knew that. Maybe Nonna's matchmaking was God's way of finding him a partner, someone who'd help him fulfill his dream of building a loving family. Lacey wasn't the only woman in the world, despite what his heart said.

Halfway down the stairs, he caught his breath.

There was Lacey in a sleeveless blue dress that highlighted her figure and her coloring. She stood in front of an ornamental mirror, attempting to fasten a necklace.

Breathe. She's not for you.

He walked slowly the rest of the way down

the stairs, watching her struggle with the small clasp. "Need some help?"

"Oh! Um, sure." She held out the ends of the necklace, her back to him, bowing her head.

Her neck looked slender and vulnerable. Her short hair brushed his fingers, soft and light as bird feathers.

He could smell her sweet, spicy perfume. *Breathe.*

He fumbled a little with the tiny clasp, dropped one end, had to start over. "Sorry. Big fingers." But that wasn't really the problem. He knew how to fasten a necklace; he'd been doing it for his women friends forever.

Why did it feel so different with Lacey?

Why was he going slowly on purpose, trying to extend the moment, to stay close to her?

He finished and stepped back quickly, forbidding his hands to linger on her shoulders. "Whoever you're meeting tonight is going to be very happy."

She turned toward him, a smile curving

her lips as she gave him an undisguised once-over. "Your date will be, too."

He laughed a little, shook his head. "My date is going to be in for a surprise, but not such a pleasant one."

"You look good, Vito." She reached up and, with one finger, touched his face. The bad side of it. "Except that there's a little shaving cream…right…here."

Their eyes met and her touch lingered on his face.

That soft, small finger, touching a place no one had ever touched, except in a medical capacity, made him suck in a breath. "It's hard to shave with…this." He gestured toward the ridged, scarred side of his face.

She let her hand open to cup his cheek. "I'm sure."

The moment lingered. He felt like he couldn't look away from Lacey's steady, light brown eyes.

Until Nonna opened her door and clapped her hands. From her room came strains of opera music. "Don't you both look gorgeous!"

Vito took a step backward and Lacey let her hand fall to her side.

"We clean up okay," he said, clearing his throat, trying to keep his cool. "How are we going to know our dates?"

"It's all set up at the restaurant."

Vito bit back a sigh and slid his hands into his pockets. "You're not going to tell us who, are you?"

"And spoil the anticipation? Of course not. That's just one of the things that will be unique about my matchmaking service. Now, you two had better get going."

That brought up another angle he hadn't considered. "Would it be awkward if we walked together to dates with other people?" he asked Lacey. "Or would you rather drive, with those heels?" *Which look spectacular*, he thought but didn't say.

"They're wedges—they're fine." Her cheeks were a little pinker than usual. "Um, sure, we can walk."

So they strolled together through the downtown of Rescue River, all dressed up. The evening air was warm, and shouts from the park indicated that families were enjoying the evening. Vito leaned just a little closer to Lacey to catch another whiff of her perfume, wishing with all his heart that he could spend this evening with her, as her date.

His thoughts toward his old friend Gerry, who'd made him promise to keep Charlie's parentage a secret, were becoming more uncharitable by the minute. The man had been a hero and a friend, and Vito mourned the loss of him, but he couldn't deny resenting the promise that stood like a wall between him and the woman he was coming to care for more each day.

"Who do you think our dates are?" she asked, looking up at him with laughter in her eyes. "Will it be people we know or complete strangers?"

"Bound to be people we know. It's Rescue River. And Nonna knows the same people we do." He actually hoped it was someone who knew what he looked like, just to spare himself the awkward moment that often happened when people met him for the first time.

They approached Chez la Ferme to discover a small crowd of people waiting outside. "Looks like they're backed up. Hope Nonna really did make a reservation."

"Or not." Lacey made a wry face. "I do have that paint can waiting for me at home."

He chuckled. She wasn't any more into this whole game than he was. "Look, there's Daisy."

"And Dion." Vito lifted an eyebrow. Were the police chief and the social worker officially admitting they were a couple? Because being together at Chez la Ferme pretty much guaranteed that they'd be perceived that way.

"Hey!" Lacey hugged both of them, first Daisy, then Dion. "Long wait?"

"Not if you let them know you're here." Dion punched Vito's arm lightly. "Get with the program, my brother."

So Vito walked in to the hostess stand and gave his name.

"Oh, yes, Mr. D'Angelo. We've been expecting you." The hostess gave him a broad smile. "Your table will be ready in just a few minutes."

Obviously, she was in on Nonna's secret.

Almost as soon as he'd exited the restaurant, while he was still walking toward his friends, the hostess came behind him. "Dion Coleman?" she called. "And Lacey McPherson?"

A slow smile crossed Dion's face. "Oh, your grandma," he said to Vito, shaking his head. And then he crooked his arm for Lacey. "Shall we?"

Lacey's eyebrows lifted as she looked up at the police chief. "Well, okay, then." She took his arm and the two of them turned toward the restaurant.

Vito's stomach seemed to drop to his toes as he watched the pair. He couldn't help noticing the details: the large squared-off college ring that glinted against Dion's dark skin, the expensive cut of his suit, the suave way he put a hand on the small of Lacey's back to guide her inside.

They were good-looking enough that several people in the crowd turned to watch. Or maybe the raised eyebrows were because Dion was linked with Daisy in the town's collective, gossipy mind.

Vito had known he couldn't be with Lacey himself, on account of Charlie. He'd almost—not quite, but almost—accepted that.

What he hadn't anticipated was how seeing Lacey with someone else would feel like a punch in the stomach.

And he should have known, because it had happened before, with Gerry. This exact same feeling: *You're not going to get her. She's going to choose someone else. And you're going to have to stand there and be a man about it. Do the right thing.*

Speaking of doing the right thing, he was being rude to Daisy, standing there watching Lacey and Dion disappear inside the restaurant like a hungry dog, tongue hanging out.

He schooled his expression before he

turned to Daisy. Was that a similar look on her face?

That brought him out of himself. He couldn't have Lacey, and it was wrong to think she should save herself for him, that she shouldn't find happiness with someone else. Dion was a good man, respected by everyone in town.

And now, he needed to go through with the evening's plans as if he didn't feel gut-shot. He didn't know Daisy well, but he assumed that if Dion was set up with Lacey, Daisy was probably set up with him. He turned to her. "Any chance you're here for a blind date, too? Set up by my grandma?"

"Yeah." She nodded. She didn't look enthusiastic.

He soldiered on, as he'd been trained to do. "Well, you didn't get the prize," he said, "but you'll get a good dinner. I think I'm your date."

"Oh. Okay." She didn't sound thrilled, but not horrified, either. "What do you mean, not the prize?"

He gestured vaguely toward the scarred side of his face. "Only a doting grandma could love this mug."

She didn't deny the ugliness of his scars, but she shrugged them away. "Most women care more about what's inside. Whereas men…" She trailed off, and then glanced down at her own curvy body. "I'm not the prize, either, compared to her." She gestured toward the door through which Dion and Lacey had disappeared.

It was true. Vito didn't find Daisy as attractive as he found Lacey. But then, he didn't find *any* woman that attractive. For better or worse, his heart had attached itself to Lacey, and he was realizing more every minute that his wasn't the kind of heart that could easily change directions. Still, Daisy—blonde, vivacious and with a killer smile—was something of a showstopper herself. And he wasn't going to be rude to her. "You *are* a prize. Anyone with any sense would wonder how someone like me got to go out with a knockout like you. I'm honored to be your date."

The crowd by the door was thinning out, and a bench opened up. "Want to sit down?"

So they sat, and talked about her work in social services, and his desire to become a teacher. She was a good conversationalist, easy to talk to. He found himself confessing his worries about scaring kids, his desire to work with them in person, and his pretty-sure decision to go with online teaching. When the hostess called them to go inside, she had to do it several times, apparently, from her expression when she came out to get them.

As they followed her into the restaurant, replete with stained glass and low lighting and good smells of bread and prime rib, they kept talking.

"Don't do online teaching if your heart is in the real classroom," she urged him as they crossed the restaurant behind the maître d'. "Kids respond to the whole person, not just how you look. I used to worry about them teasing me about my weight, but they're completely fine with it."

"As are most men," he assured her. "Women think we all like stick-skinny women, but that's not the case. You're beautiful."

"Your table, sir." The maître d' gestured, and Vito held Daisy's chair for her.

Only then did he realize that Dion and Lacey were just around a small corner from them, probably within earshot of most things they would say.

Not only that, but the two of them were leaning toward each other, sharing an appetizer and appearing to have a marvelous time.

Chapter Ten

Lacey looked at the handsome man across the table from her and tried to ignore Vito and Daisy being seated practically right behind them.

Unfortunately, she couldn't ignore what she'd heard. "You're a beautiful woman," Vito had said to Daisy.

Which was true, and she didn't begrudge Daisy the praise, but the way it stung alerted her to something she hadn't quite realized before: she wanted Vito for herself.

"Hey," Dion said. "What's going on?"

She shrugged and toyed with her water glass.

"All of a sudden you're not comfortable," he said. "Is it something I said?"

"No! No, you're fine. What were we talking about?" She laughed nervously. "I'm sorry, I'm a little intimidated."

His forehead creased. "Intimidated? Why?"

"You're kind of known for your wisdom," she said, "not to mention that you're the police chief."

"Which is all a nice way of saying I'm an old man," he said, "who's fortunate to be out with a fine-looking young woman."

The words were gallant, but Lacey could tell Dion wasn't interested in her in *that* way. Rather than feeling insulted, she felt relieved and suddenly more comfortable. This was a little awkward, especially with Vito and Daisy so close, but at least she knew she wasn't misleading Dion.

"I'm the fortunate one," she said. "I might pick your brain about some Bible stuff. You're said to know everything there is to know."

"Who says that?"

"Angelica's husband, Troy. He thinks you're the font of all wisdom. And my brother's a fan, too."

"Don't you be thinking I'm perfect," he warned. "Nobody's perfect. Nobody's even close, right? That's what the good book says."

"See, you're making my point for me, quoting scripture at the drop of a hat." She frowned. "Anyway, of course, you're right. But I've spent my whole life trying to be good. Trying to be perfect."

"We all try," he said, "and that's not bad."

She did her best to ignore the rumble of Vito's voice behind her, but it played along her nerve endings like an instrument. She forced it away, forced herself to talk with Dion about her brother, with whom he'd had a good deal of official contact until Buck had dried out and they'd become friends. She forced herself to rave over the delicious, beautifully presented food: Dion's prime rib, her own organic grilled salmon.

"That was great," she said when they'd pushed away their plates.

"Yes, it was," he said, "but let me ask you something. Are you in this matchmaking thing for real?"

She looked at him and slowly shook her head. "Not really. I'm just doing it for Nonna. You?" She only asked the question to be polite, because she was pretty sure of the answer. "I always heard you were with Daisy."

"Everyone thinks that," he said, smoothly changing the subject. "You're a newish widow. It makes sense you're not ready to do a lot of dating."

"Yeah. I… I really loved my husband."

Dion didn't say, "He was a good guy." That would normally be the remark you made, wouldn't it? But instead, he said, "That's obvious. Gerry was blessed to have you. But—" he raised a finger and pinned her with a steady gaze "—at some point, you're going to have to move on. You're too young of a woman to give up on life."

She wasn't going to tell him about her infertility. Instead, she turned the tables. "Do you take your own advice?"

Dion cocked his head to one side, smiling at her. "Touché. I've been on my own a lot longer than you have, and I should probably be letting go of some baggage by now."

She wanted to ask him about his past, but the way his face closed when he mentioned it told her she shouldn't. "Moving on isn't as easy as it sounds, is it?"

"No," he said. "But let your feelings lead and you'll be fine. Your feelings and your heart. And most of all, the Lord."

Well, if she were to let her feelings lead... Involuntarily, she glanced over at Vito and then back at Dion. "I'm ashamed to say that I haven't spent much time consulting the Lord about this," she admitted.

The server took their plates away and promised to be right back with the dessert tray. "There's no time like the present," Dion said, "to take it to the Lord. Want to?"

So she let him take her hand in his, closed her eyes, listened to Dion's quiet words and said a few herself. Asked for forgiveness that she'd neglected to seek God's guidance in her feelings. Asked Him to lead her in the right direction.

When they were finished, she felt cleansed.

"And now," Dion said, "if we can get their attention, do you think we should move our table together with our friends for dessert?"

"I, um, I don't know if Nonna would approve."

"Nonna's not here, is she? Hey, Vito." Dion caught his attention and made the suggestion, and the servers rushed to help, assuring them it was no problem.

Once they were all sitting together, there was a slightly awkward silence, broken by the approach of the dessert tray. The waiter began to describe the offerings.

Lacey looked over at Daisy. "I need chocolate. Now. You?"

"I agree."

After a restless night, Vito woke Charlie up early, figuring they'd grab breakfast and go burn off some energy on the basketball court. But even before they reached the main floor of the guesthouse, delicious smells of cinnamon and bread wafted toward them.

Could Lacey be up baking cinnamon rolls?

But when they walked into the kitchen, there was Nonna in her Kiss the Cook apron, bending over to check on something in the oven and looking like her old self.

At the table was Miss Minnie Falcon, matriarch of the Senior Towers and former Sunday school teacher to almost every child in Rescue River. Next to her was Lou Ann Miller, stirring sugar into a cup of coffee.

"You're looking good, Nonna," he said, walking over to the stove and giving his grandmother a kiss.

"And that smells good!" Charlie came over as Nonna removed the pan from the oven. "Can I have some?"

"Five minutes, *cùcciolo*." She patted Charlie's shoulder, smiling.

Vito felt a great weight lifting off him, a weight he hadn't known he was carrying.

Nonna was going to be okay. Suddenly he could see it and feel it and believe it. Not only that, but she'd called Charlie by the same affectionate name she used to use on Vito and his brother. That, more than anything, meant Charlie was becoming part of their family. He swallowed against a sudden tightness in his throat and walked over to greet the ladies at the table.

As good as her word, Nonna brought a steaming loaf of cinnamon bread, along with small cups of butter and jam, and placed them in the middle of the table.

"Italian breakfast like the old days." Vito put an arm around Nonna, still feeling a little misty-eyed.

Charlie's hand froze in the act of grabbing a piece of the bread. "Why is it brown?" he asked.

"Because I used the healthy flour. It tastes just as good, so eat up."

Charlie grabbed a piece, slathered it with butter and jam and took a huge bite before anyone else had even secured a piece. "It's good, Nonna," he said, his mouth full of food.

Vito leaned close to Charlie's ear. "Good table manners will get you more food," he whispered.

Charlie raised his eyebrows. "What'd I do?"

"Don't talk with your mouth full." They'd cover the grabby behavior later. First things first.

Miss Minnie put a clawlike hand on Vito's arm. "I understand you were our first matchmaking client," she said.

"Yes, tell us all about it." Lou Ann Miller raised a slice of bread to her nose and inhaled, closing her eyes. "Fabulous, dear. You've outdone yourself."

As Nonna beamed, the door from the backyard opened and Lacey breezed in. She wore a red-and-white-checkered shirt and cutoff shorts and she looked as carefree as she had at twelve.

And he was a goner.

"That smells amazing, Nonna D'Angelo,"

she said, approaching the table. "And look, whole grains! I'm impressed."

"Hey, Miss Lacey, you're not wearing your necklace."

Lacey's hand flew to her throat. "Oh, wow, I'll run up and get it before I eat."

"Want me to get it for you?" The words were out of Vito's mouth before he realized that he didn't, in fact, want to get her the necklace. Didn't want her to wear Gerry's wedding ring around her neck anymore.

"Oh, it's okay. I'll get it." She half walked, half skipped out of the kitchen.

"My Vito." Nonna pinched his cheek—the second time someone had touched his scars in the past two days. "Always too nice for your own good."

"That's right," Miss Minnie said unexpectedly. "Being kind isn't all there is to life. Take a stand!"

"What are you ladies talking about?"

Lou Ann Miller glanced over at Charlie, who'd grabbed his handheld game and was immersed in it, still chewing on a huge mouthful of bread. She turned back to Vito. "Your love life is what we're talking about."

Vito looked from Lou Ann to his grandmother to Miss Minnie. "Seriously? Is that what I'm doing wrong? Being kind and nice?" But of course, they didn't know about his Charlie deception, which wasn't nice at all.

"Tell us about last night," Nonna said instead of answering his question. She removed her apron and sat down at the table and looked up at him expectantly.

"It was…fine. Daisy is great."

"And you don't want to date her."

"Well, of course he doesn't. For one thing, she's attached to Dion Coleman at the hip."

"And then there's the fact that Vito's affections are elsewhere."

"That's obvious. The question is what can we do about it?"

The three women's conversation was spinning out of control. "Nobody needs to do anything about it," he protested. "I can handle my own life."

The only good thing was that Charlie wasn't listening; he was just eating bread and playing with his game.

Lacey came back into the room and Vito didn't know whether to be glad or sorry. He got busy cleaning up the breakfast dishes and washing mixing bowls and bread pans.

"How was your date with Dion?" Lou Ann asked her.

Vito couldn't help tuning his ears to hear what she would say. They'd all ended the evening together, on a friendly note and laughing about various people's efforts to play matchmaker over the years, but Vito still had a sinking feeling he couldn't compete with Dion, suave and good-looking and successful.

And he *couldn't* compete, he reminded himself. He couldn't have Lacey, because telling her the truth would destroy her world. Destroy her image of the husband whose ring she wore around her neck.

"It was great," she said easily. "He's a lot less intimidating on a date than when he's being the police chief. Mmmm, this bread is good."

Vito glanced over to see three gray heads turn toward Lacey. "So," Nonna said, "do you like Dion?"

"She means *like* like," Charlie supplied, his mouth full. "Like a boyfriend."

It seemed like everyone in the room—except Charlie—was holding their breath.

"No, I don't think so." Lacey seemed unconscious of how much interest her words were generating. "And I don't think he likes me that way, either, but I'm glad to get to know him better as a friend. He's a good guy and a wonderful Christian."

Vito let out a breath and his tight shoulders relaxed. He grabbed a dish towel and started drying cutlery with great energy.

"I'm not really ready to date," she continued, fingering her necklace. "I'm afraid you're going to have to find some other clients."

There was a little commotion outside the door, and then it opened, framing Buck,

Gina and little Bobby, who toddled across the room toward Lacey. "Laasss," he crowed reverently, crashing into her leg and hanging on.

"Hi, honey!" She lifted him onto her lap and tickled his stomach, making him laugh.

She looked beautiful with a baby.

She would look beautiful with *his* baby.

Man, he had it bad and he had to stop.

"Mind if the dogs come in, Lace?" Buck asked.

She glanced down at Mr. Whiskers. "Run while you can, buddy," she said, and then beckoned for Gina to let the dogs in.

Immediately, Crater, a large black mutt with a deep scar on his back, galloped in. At his heels was a small white mop of a dog, barking joyously.

Charlie threw himself out of the chair and started rolling and roughhousing with them.

Vito looked at the ladies to see if they found the ruckus disturbing, but they were watching and laughing. Bobby struggled out of Lacey's lap and toddled fearlessly into the fray.

Buck and Gina came over to the table and talked above the kids and dogs, and all the noise created a dull roar Vito couldn't really follow, given his hearing loss. His aids worked well with individual conversations, but big noisy groups were still a challenge.

He was wiping down counters when Charlie came over and tugged at his arm. He bent down to hear what the boy had to say.

"Can we get a dog now, Dad?"

That had been predictable. "Of these two, which kind do you like?"

"Can we get two?"

"No!"

"Then, I like the big one. Can we get one like that? With cool scars?"

The phrasing made Vito lift an eyebrow. Cool scars, huh? That scars could be cool was a new concept to him. "We'll start thinking about it more seriously," he promised.

Given how strong his feelings for Lacey

had become, he had some serious thinking of his own to do, as well.

When there was a knock on the front door, Lacey hurried to answer it, relieved to escape the busy kitchen and the probing questions of Nonna D'Angelo, Miss Minnie and Lou Ann. Not to mention Vito's thoughtful eyes.

It was Daisy. "Hey, I was walking by, and I thought I'd take the chance that you were here. Do you have a minute?"

"Um, sure." She and Daisy knew each other, but they weren't drop-in friends. She came out on the porch and gestured toward a rocking chair, tucking her feet under herself in the porch swing. "What's up?"

"I just wanted to make sure we're okay about last night."

Lacey forced a laugh. "We were clearly all victims of the grandma matchmaking brigade. What happened isn't your fault or mine, or any of ours."

"And it was fun in the end, right?"

"Sure." As she thought back, she realized that it *had* been fun, sitting and laughing with Vito and Daisy and Dion. Except for that nagging anxiety at the pit of her stomach.

Daisy was watching her, eyes narrowed. "But…" she prompted.

Lacey shrugged. "Nothing."

"It's not nothing. I *knew* something was bugging you last night. What's going on?"

"Nothing's going on." She paused. "If you're worried about whether I like Dion, I do, but not as a boyfriend."

Daisy waved a hand. "I know. I could tell. And it's not my business, anyway. I *wish* Dion would meet someone."

Lacey lifted an eyebrow, but didn't comment. She couldn't tell if Daisy meant it or not.

"And I'm not interested in Vito that way, either."

Lacey tried to school her facial expression, but she couldn't help feeling happy. "I…wasn't sure."

"I mean, he's great," Daisy said, "but I'm pretty sure he only has eyes for you."

Lacey had thought she couldn't get any more joyous, but an extra wave of it washed over her at Daisy's words. "You really think so?"

Daisy nodded. "I sat and had dinner with him, and he was great, he really was. So nice and flattering and kind. But he couldn't stop himself from looking over at you guys every time you and Dion laughed."

A breathless feeling took Lacey over then. Maybe this—her and Vito—could really happen. Maybe it would. "Do you think it's wrong for me to think about another man, so soon after losing Gerry? As a social worker, I mean?"

Daisy studied her thoughtfully. "It's been over a year, right?"

She nodded.

"And what have you done to get over the loss?"

"Well…" Lacey thought about it. "I've had counseling, with a psychologist and with Pastor Ricky. And with some of my friends, too, unofficially. I'm doing desensitizing things about kids, because…did you know I lost a baby, too?" She was amazed that she could say the words openly now, with only an ache instead of a sharp, horrific pain.

Daisy nodded. "I heard, and I'm sorry for your loss. That must have been terribly hard to deal with."

"Well…yeah. The worst. And I never thought I'd heal, but Buck, and little Bobby, and the church… Lots of people have helped me, and life goes on."

The door flew open and Charlie emerged. He threw his arms around Lacey and said into her ear: "I think Dad's getting me a dog!" Then he ran down the stairs and across the street to the basketball hoop where a couple of neighborhood kids were playing.

Lacey looked after him and blinked. "That came out of nowhere. I thought he didn't like me."

"If you seem to pose a threat to his relationship with Vito, he may act out. On the other hand, he might very well need a mother figure." Daisy leaned back in the chair, rocking gently.

"A mother figure?" Lacey laughed. "Why would he think of me that way? I'm not even dating his dad."

"Yet. Charlie may see something that the two of you won't yet acknowledge."

Heat suffused Lacey's cheeks and she didn't know how to respond. Because the truth was, she was interested in dating Vito. After last night, watching him with Daisy, she was sure of it.

There was a fumbling sound at the door and Miss Minnie Falcon made her way out, struggling a little with her rolling walker. Both Lacey and Daisy jumped up to help her.

"Would you like to sit a spell on your old porch?" Lacey asked. She'd bought the house from Miss Minnie two years ago when it had become too much for her to handle, and she tried to encourage the older woman to maintain her connection. It made Miss Minnie happy, and as her brother's wife, Gina, had discovered, Miss Minnie and the house itself were full of stories. Besides, Lacey enjoyed the sharp-tongued woman's company.

"Thank you, dear. I wouldn't mind."

Lacey made sure Miss Minnie was settled comfortably while Daisy folded her walker and put it against the porch railing.

"It got a little too noisy in that kitchen. I like children, but in controlled circumstances."

"I hear you," Daisy said. "It's probably just as well I don't have children." Then Daisy's eyes went round and she looked at Lacey apologetically. "I'm sorry. I guess this is a sensitive topic for you."

"Kind of," Lacey said. Then, to her own surprise, she added, "Especially since I can't have kids."

"Never?" Daisy's eyes widened, and she reached out to give Lacey's hand a quick squeeze.

"That's what they say." She lowered her

head, and then looked from one woman to the other. "Please don't tell anyone, okay? I... I'm still getting used to it. And it's not common knowledge."

"It shouldn't be," Miss Minnie said, her voice a little sharp. "Young people share far too much about themselves these days. Some things are simply private."

Daisy laughed. "I take it you're not baring your soul on social media, Miss Minnie?"

"My, no." The older woman turned back toward Lacey. "There are other ways to nurture children, besides bearing them."

Lacey opened her mouth to disagree, and then realized she was wrong. Miss Minnie knew what she was talking about from personal experience. "You taught Sunday school for almost all the kids in Rescue River, so I guess you're right. That's one way."

"And you're sure getting close with Charlie, from the looks of things," Daisy said. "Kids need all kinds of people in their lives to grow up right. Not just their parents." She turned to Miss Minnie. "Did you ever regret not having kids?"

Lacey flinched a little. That was definitely a personal question. Daisy was the type to ask them, but Miss Minnie was the type to offer a sharp reply.

"Not that it's commonly known, but of course I did," the older woman said. "That's the reason I taught Sunday school all those years. If you don't have a family, you have to do a little more figuring to build a good life for yourself."

"You may not have much family, but I hear you do have a boyfriend," Daisy said slyly.

Lacey smiled, remembering what she'd seen at the Chatterbox. "Mr. Love, right?"

"You young people and your gossip tire me out. I need to get back home." But a faint blush colored Miss Minnie's cheeks.

"We're sorry." Lacey stood to help the woman to her feet. "We don't mean to tease. It's just nice to see…" She paused to clarify her own thoughts. "It's nice to see a single person having a fun, active social life."

"That's right," Daisy contributed, picking up Miss Minnie's walker. "We single ladies have to stick together. And what's more, it's crazy that any time you're friends with a man, people start linking you up romantically."

Lacey and Miss Minnie glanced at each other as they made their way down the steps. Was Daisy talking about Dion? Was she or wasn't she involved with him?

After they'd walked Miss Minnie back to the Senior Towers, they stopped on the sidewalk to talk before parting ways.

"You going to the fireworks tonight?" Lacey asked.

"Yeah, I love the Fourth of July. You?"

Lacey shrugged. "I'll probably watch them from the front porch, with Nonna."

"And Vito?"

"Stop trying to match-make," Lacey scolded. "You heard what Miss Minnie said. We all share too much about our personal lives." But even saying that felt hypocritical, because the thought of Vito, of watching fireworks under the stars together, made a delicious excitement fill her chest. "I'm sure he and Charlie will watch the fireworks, one way or another."

"Then I'm sure you'll enjoy plenty of fireworks," Daisy teased.

"Hey, now!" She watched the woman— who was maybe going to become a closer friend—wave and stroll down the street.

A fluttery excitement filled her. Maybe it *would* be a night to remember.

Or maybe not. She herself was starting to feel like a relationship with Vito might be possible. But she wasn't sure how he felt. With Vito, it always seemed to be one step forward, one step back.

Chapter Eleven

On Monday afternoon, Vito was tempted to turn down his hearing aids as he drove home from the dog rescue with Charlie and his new dog going crazy in the back. Had he just made a big mistake? What was Lacey going to think of this new, and very loud, guest?

At a stop sign, he looked back to check on them. Wolfie, the new white husky mix, stood eager in the giant crate Troy had lent them, bungee-corded in place in the bed of the pickup. Charlie was turned around as far as his seat belt would allow, poking at the dog through the open back window, talking nonsense to it, turning back toward Vito to shout "look at him, *look* at him." The disbelieving thrill in his voice and his eyes melted Vito's heart.

Whatever the challenges, he thanked God that he could do this for Charlie.

When they pulled into the guesthouse driveway, Lacey was outside on her knees, weeding the narrow flower garden that fronted the house. Dressed in old jeans and gardening gloves, she looked up and smiled, brushing blond bangs out of her eyes with the back of her hand.

Vito felt an unbelievable warmth just looking at her.

They'd finally relaxed around each other, watching the fireworks together, eating Nonna's new, healthy concoctions, hanging around the house. Homey, domestic stuff. It was dangerous territory, but he couldn't resist reveling in it for a little while, at least.

He stopped the truck, and Charlie jumped out. "Miss Lacey, Miss Lacey, come see my new dog!"

She stood easily and pressed her hands to the small of her back, smiling, then headed toward the vehicle where Vito was opening the back hatch. "I can't wait to meet him!"

Vito opened the hatch and the crate, and Wolfie bounded out. He leaped up on Lacey, his paws almost to her shoulders, nearly knocking her down. Then he ran through the yard in circles, barking, his big feet tearing at Lacey's flowers. Finally, he approached Charlie in a play bow, his blue eyes dancing, his mouth open in a laughing pant.

"Sorry, sorry!" Vito ran to hook the new leash on to Wolfie's collar, but the dog darted away.

Charlie tackled the dog, and the two of them rolled on the ground together like a couple of puppies, while Vito struggled to find the ring on the dog's collar to hook on the leash.

Finally, he attached the leash and put the looped end in Charlie's hand. "Hold on to him!" he told Charlie, and then stepped back beside Lacey to watch the pair. "I'm sorry about your garden. I'll fix it. He's a little excited."

"So what happened to the concept of a small dog?" she asked drily.

Vito inhaled the scent of wild roses that seemed to come from Lacey's hair. "I know. I'm sorry. I should have called to make sure a bigger dog was okay. It's just… We were playing with a bunch of the dogs, and it was as if they chose each other."

"He was the one, Lacey! Isn't he cool?" Charlie rose to his knees as the dog bounded around him in circles, barking.

A smile tugged at the corner of Lacey's mouth, and in that moment, Vito saw her tenderness for Charlie and fell a little bit more in love with her.

"Well…we did have Crater here, and he was as big as…what's this guy's name?"

"Wolfie!" Charlie shouted, pouncing on the dog again.

"Hold tight to that leash while I get his stuff out," Vito warned, and then turned back to the truck and started unloading dog food and dishes. Rather than an expensive dog bed, they'd stopped by the Goodwill store; a big blanket would do for the dog to sleep on.

He was carrying it all up to the porch when Nonna came out.

"What have we here?" she asked, smiling.

"It's Charlie's new dog." Vito looked over in time to see the dog pull out of Charlie's grip and head for the porch.

Before Vito could do anything, Lacey dived for the leash and held on. The dog actually pulled her for a couple of feet before she was able to stop it. "Sit, Wolfie!" she commanded, but the dog just cocked his head at her, his mouth open in what looked like a laugh.

Lacey sat up cross-legged and held the leash firmly. "Nonna, this dog's a little crazy. Make sure you're sitting down when he's around, and wear long pants until he settles down." To Vito she added, "He's strong and he's got big claws. He could knock Nonna down in a second, and those claws could scratch her up pretty bad."

"He knocked me down," Charlie said, almost proudly. "And he scratched me, too." He held up an arm. Even from this distance, Vito could see the thin line of blood.

They'd definitely start training Wolfie today.

"Why was Wolfie at the shelter?" he heard Lacey ask Charlie. "He looks like a purebred, and he acts like a puppy."

"He's two years old, and the people who had him said he was un, un…" He looked up at Vito.

"Unmanageable?" Lacey asked drily.

"That's it!"

Lacey rolled her eyes at Vito, looking exactly like she had as a teenager.

He put down the supplies and spread his hands. "I know. I know, and I'm sorry. It was just something in his eyes."

"Wolfie's, or Charlie's?"

"Both. Charlie fell in love with Wolfie as soon as he saw him, for whatever reason."

He noticed the "I found a home" placard they'd gotten at the shelter. "Supposedly, we have two weeks to test everything out. If he doesn't work for us, we can choose another dog."

"And two other families tried him and he didn't work out, so he was really sad," Charlie said. "I hope we can keep him. We can keep him, can't we, Dad?"

Vito blew out a breath. "We're going to do our best to give him a good home. With love and attention and discipline, he should settle down."

"Like me," Charlie said offhandedly, and went to hug Wolfie. "Don't worry, guy. Dad let *me* stay."

Lacey's hand flew to her mouth and Vito felt his throat tighten. They glanced at each other, and it was as if they agreed without words: this *had* to work.

His phone buzzed in his pocket, and seeing that the dog was safely under Lacey's control, he pulled it out for a quick look.

He didn't recognize the number, but it

was local. "Hey, I'd better take this just in case it's about a job," he said to Lacey. "Can you…" He waved a hand at Charlie, the new dog and Nonna.

"Got it," she said instantly. "Come on, Charlie. Let's see if we can teach him how to walk nicely on a leash."

The fact that she had his back so readily and without complaint made Vito's heart swell with gratitude. He clicked on the call.

"Vito D'Angelo? This is Sandra Sutherland, head of the school district's summer programs. You interviewed with one of my people last week."

"That's right." He sank down onto the porch step to focus. "What's up?"

"I'd like to talk to you about a job opening for this summer, with a possibility of extending into fall. How are you with special needs boys? Older, say from eight to sixteen?"

Without even thinking about it, he laughed. "That's getting to be my specialty." He looked down the street at Charlie.

She went on to detail the job of Vito's dreams: part-time for now, sports centered, mentoring and counseling a small group four mornings per week. "We thought you'd be perfect for it."

"Can I ask why?"

She spoke slowly, thoughtfully. "Your background as a veteran, your leadership experience and the fact that you're familiar with the foster care system all play into it. And..." She hesitated.

Why would she sound so uncomfortable? Even as he thought of the question, Vito's hand went to his face and he knew the answer. "Do some of the kids have physical disabilities? Visible ones?"

"That's it," she said, sounding relieved. "We actually have two boys, siblings, who were in a terrible house fire. They lost their mother, and they have some disfiguring burns. They've been acting out, even within the small group, so when Marnie came to me and said she had a good interview with you, and she mentioned your scars..."

Vito blew out a breath and looked skyward. Was this what God was doing? He'd never thought his scarred face would be an asset.

"Look, if you're interested and available, we could set up a time to talk. Sooner rather than later, though. Their current group leader just quit."

He couldn't help chuckling again. Between Charlie, and Wolfie the dog, and these boys, it looked like he was headed toward a career in rehab. "I'm free later today," he said, and they set up a time.

He clicked his phone off and just sat a minute, thinking.

He wanted a career in education, with children. But with his looks, he'd figured he couldn't do anything but online teaching. Now, come to find out, there was a perfect job within reach—partly *because* of how he looked.

Special ed. Physical limitations. He hadn't thought about it before, but he was definitely strong enough to lift kids in and out of wheelchairs. At the VA, he'd gotten to know guys with all kinds of disabilities. And with his own very visible scars, the students would know instantly that he understood.

Father God, You work in mysterious ways.

His heart beating faster, he looked down the street and saw Lacey and Charlie coming back toward the house, laughing, trying to manage the unruly Wolfie. He stood up and headed toward them. He wanted nothing more than to tell Lacey the good news.

A job, Charlie, and maybe Lacey. Everything he wanted was within reach. Under one condition: he had to figure out a way to tell Lacey the truth about Charlie.

Lacey looked up from trying to contain Wolfie's enthusiasm and saw Vito walking toward them, face alight with some kind of excitement. The call he'd gotten must have been good news.

"Dad! Dad!" Charlie bounced toward Vito, leaving Lacey to try to hold Wolfie back with both hands as he lunged after the boy he seemed to know already was his.

Vito ruffled Charlie's hair. "How's it going? We better help Lacey, huh?"

They came toward her and Vito took hold of the out-of-control dog's leash. "We need to figure out how to work off some of his energy," he said.

"That's what me and Lacey were trying to do! Only, he's so crazy and he doesn't know how to walk on a leash and he ran after a squirrel and we almost couldn't hold on!"

"He's excited, buddy. We'd better let him run in the yard at the guesthouse, if that's okay with Lacey."

"Good idea," she said. "He was about to yank my arm off!"

Once they'd gotten him inside the fence, they all ran and played with him. It didn't take long to discover that the fence had a broken section; Charlie and Lacey ran after the dog and brought him back while Vito did a makeshift fix. After Wolfie's energy finally started to calm, Vito and Lacey sat down on a bench together while Charlie lay beside the dog, holding tightly to his leash.

"So, finally I can ask. What had you looking so excited after that phone call?"

Vito's face lit up. "I might have a job."

As he told her about the offer, Lacey nodded. It sounded perfect for someone as nurturing—and strong—as Vito.

"I'm going to have to set up some doggie day care for Wolfie, I think, and Charlie has his park program, so we'll be out of your hair a little more if this all works out."

She tilted her head to one side, studying him. "You're the least self-centered guy I know."

He looked blank. "What do you mean?"

"Most men would be crowing and bragging about getting a job, but you're all about how to take care of your responsibilities and how it'll affect other people. That's…refreshing."

His eyes narrowed. "You sound like you've had some experience with another type of guy."

She looked at the ground, nodding, feeling guilty. Lately she'd been having some realizations that were altering her view of her marriage, and it wasn't at all comfortable.

"Gerry?"

She hesitated a moment. But she could tell Vito, couldn't she? "Yes. I hate to say it, but he tended to think of himself first. When the time came to reenlist, he didn't even ask me—he just did it and bragged about it. And I was pregnant!"

"You're kidding. That wasn't right. You deserved better." He touched her chin, forcing her to look at him. "You deserve the very best."

She met his warm brown eyes and her heart beat faster. She didn't know about deserving the very best, but she had the feeling that being with Vito would *be* the very best. Maybe even, in some ways, better than being with Gerry. It was a disloyal thought that made her look away from Vito, but that lingered in her mind long into the night.

* * *

Two days later, Vito set out lawn chairs at the lake and pulled a picnic lunch—courtesy of the Chatterbox Café—out of the back of the pickup.

It was his way of making it up to Lacey for all the hassles of having a giant new dog in her guesthouse. He'd talked her into taking the day off with them—his last day off for a while, as his new job started tomorrow.

"I wish we could've brought Wolfie," Charlie said, his face pouty as he reluctantly helped unload the picnic basket. Since Monday, he and the dog had been inseparable.

"This is a good way to test out the doggie day care where he's going to spend mornings. And Lacey needs a break."

Charlie made a face, and Vito sighed. The boy and Lacey had been getting along great, but when he was in a bad mood, he tended to take it out on everyone. He hadn't wanted to come to the lake because it meant being separated from Wolfie. And probably because Vito's new job started tomorrow. Even though it wouldn't mean much of an adjustment for Charlie, even though he liked his summer parks program, anything new was tough on a kid who'd had too many changes and losses in his young life.

"I'll take over if you want to check out the water," Lacey said to Charlie, coming over to the table. "Man, it's hot! I'm coming in as soon as we get our stuff set up."

She was wearing a perfectly modest black one-piece and cutoff denim shorts. With her blond hair and sun-kissed, rosy face, the combination was striking.

Very striking.

"Hey, Charlie!" came a boy's shout from the beach area.

"Xavier's here!" Charlie's bad mood dissipated instantly. "Cool!" Without asking permission, he ran down toward the water.

"Stay in the shallow part," Vito called after him. He waved to Xavier's mom, Angelica, who was sitting with several other women right at the dividing line between grass and sand. He pointed at Charlie and she nodded, indicating she'd keep an eye on him.

"Can he swim?" Lacey asked.

"Not real well. His old life wasn't conducive to swimming lessons."

She spread a red-and-white plastic tablecloth on the splintery picnic table and anchored it with mustard, ketchup and pickle bottles. "Speaking of his other life, how are his visits with his mom going?"

"Okay, when she shows up sober." She and Charlie had had two supervised visits since the first Sunday one. One of the other planned visits she'd canceled, and once, she'd shown up high, causing the social worker to nix her seeing Charlie. "Whether the visit works out or not, he gets upset. Tuesdays are rough."

"Well, let's make his Wednesday better." She flashed a brilliant smile at him as she set out a big container of lemonade. "Man, I'm hot. I'm going to go say hi to Angelica and dip in the water."

"I'll probably be down." Vito wiped his forehead on his T-shirt sleeve.

Before Iraq, he'd have whipped off his shirt and jumped in the water in a heartbeat. Now, though, he hesitated.

For one thing, he'd have to take out his hearing aids. And while he could still hear some, especially if a person spoke clearly and was close by, he couldn't keep up with conversations, especially when there was a lot of background noise.

Add to that the dark, raised scars that slashed across his chest and back, ugly reminders of the plate glass window that had exploded beside him that last violent day in Kabul. He'd taken the brunt of the glass in his chest, with a few choice gashes in his face and back.

Outside of a hospital, the only person who'd ever seen the scars on his torso was Charlie, and he'd recoiled the first time Vito had taken off his shirt in his presence.

To have a whole beach full of people do the same might be more than Vito could handle.

It wasn't that he was vain, but he hadn't yet gotten used to turning people off, scaring kids. And mostly, he couldn't stand for perfect, gorgeous Lacey to see how he looked without his shirt.

Hearing young, angry voices shouting down at the water, Vito abandoned his load of beach towels and headed toward where Charlie and Xavier seemed to be in a standoff.

"It's not *fair*." Charlie clenched a fist and got into fighting position.

"Charlie!" Vito shouted, speeding up to a run.

"Take that!" Xavier let out a banshee scream and brought his foot up in an ineffectual martial arts kick, at the same moment that Charlie tried to punch him.

Somehow, both boys ended up on the ground, which seemed to end the disagreement.

Vito reached the boys. "Hey, Charlie, you know hitting doesn't solve any problems."

Angelica came over, not looking too concerned. "Xavier. You know you're not to practice karate on your friends. You need to apologize."

"You, too, Charlie."

Identical sulky lower lips came out.

Identical mumbles of "Sorry."

Then Xavier's face brightened. "C'mon, let's get in the lake!" he yelled, and both boys scrambled to their feet and ran to the water as if nothing had happened between them.

Getting in the lake sounded really refreshing. "Sorry about that," Vito said to Angelica. "I didn't see how it started, but I'll speak to Charlie."

"Don't worry about it. These things happen with boys, and they don't last but a minute." She smiled at him. "How's Wolfie working out?"

"He's a handful," Vito said, chuckling. "Bet Troy's glad to have him off his hands."

"There's a sucker born every minute," she teased. "Actually, he's a great dog. He just needed to find the right home." She nodded toward the other women. "Come on over and say hi."

The sight of Lacey, hair slicked back, perched on the end of someone's beach chair, was all the magnet he needed. He went over and greeted Gina and a woman named Sidney. They had their chairs circled around three babies, and as he watched, little Bobby held out his arms to Lacey and she lifted him up. "Such a big boy!" she said, nuzzling his bare stomach and blowing a raspberry on it, making the toddler laugh wildly.

Vito's heart seemed to pause, then pound. Lacey looked incredible with little Bobby, like she was born to be a mother. And suddenly, Vito wished with all his heart that she could be the mother of all the children he wanted to have.

If only he could tell her the truth about Charlie, cutting away the huge secret between them, he could let her know how he felt and see if there was any chance she'd be interested in him. But telling the truth would destroy her happy illusions about her husband and her marriage. Not to mention the impact the truth would have on Charlie, if he could even understand it.

And Vito didn't take promises lightly, especially deathbed promises.

The trouble was, he was having a hard time imagining a future without Lacey in it. Somehow, in these weeks of living at the guesthouse, she'd become integral to his life and his happiness.

"Dad! Come in the water!" Charlie and Xavier were throwing a beach ball back and forth.

"You should get in." Lacey smiled up at him. "The water feels great."

The sun beat down and he was sweating hard now, partly from the heat of the day and partly from the warmth he felt inside, being here with Lacey.

"Let's take the babies down to dip their feet in the water," Angelica suggested. The other women agreed, and soon they were all at the water's edge, wading.

"You're not worried about getting burned,

are you?" Lacey asked him. "You're dark skinned. But I have some sunscreen back at the car if you need it."

"Why d'you have your shirt on, Dad?" Charlie asked, crashing into Vito as he leaped to catch the ball.

Vito's face heated, and to avoid answering, he splashed Charlie. That led to a huge splash fight and Vito was able to cool off some, even though he didn't dunk to get his shirt entirely wet. It was white, and his scars would show through.

When they got hungry, they headed back up to the picnic tables and Vito grilled hot dogs. The women and babies had declined to join them, but Xavier had come over to get a hot dog. It was fun and relaxing, just the kind of day he'd hoped they could have, a gift to Charlie and to Lacey, too.

"You nervous about starting your job tomorrow?" Lacey asked as they ate.

"A little," he admitted. "It's definitely going to be a challenge. I expect some testing."

"You'll handle it well," she reassured him. "You're great with kids."

Charlie grabbed the ketchup and squirted it on his hot dog. The bottle made a raspberry sound which Charlie immediately imitated, laughing.

"Let me do it!" Xavier cried, grabbing for the ketchup. As he tried to tug it from Charlie's hand, he accidentally squeezed the bottle. Ketchup sprayed around the table, painting a line across Charlie, Lacey and Vito's chests.

"That's enough!" Vito plucked the squirt bottle from Xavier's hand and set it at the other end of the table, away from the boys.

"I'm sorry," Xavier said, looking serious and a little frightened as he surveyed the damage.

"It looks like blood!" Charlie said. He and Xavier looked at each other. Charlie made another raspberry sound, and both boys burst out laughing.

Vito rolled his eyes. "Sorry," he said as he

handed napkins to Lacey, and dabbed at the mess on his own shirt.

She shrugged and met his eyes, her own twinkling, and he was struck again with how great she was. She didn't get bent out of shape about boys and their antics. What a partner she'd be.

"This isn't coming off, and it stinks," she announced, gesturing to the ketchup on her shirt. "I'm getting in the water. And I bet I can beat you two boys." She jumped up from the picnic table and took off.

Immediately, the boys followed her, laughing and yelling.

Vito watched from the picnic table, alone and sweating in a now-even-smellier T-shirt. More than one male head turned to watch Lacey's progress. With her short hair and petite figure, laughing with the boys, she looked like a kid. But if you took a second look—as several guys were doing—she was all woman.

He dearly wanted to take his shirt off and follow her into the water. To be an easy, relaxed part of things. A partner she could be proud of.

He let his head drop into his hands, closed his eyes and prayed for insight and help. Insight to understand what to do, and help to do the right thing. Not just now, in regards to his ultimately silly shirt dilemma, but overall, in regards to his promise.

The smell of warm ketchup got to him, though, and he lifted his head again without any answers.

Except a memory from his time rehabing at the VA: had *he* ever lost esteem for someone because they had scars?

And the answer was glaringly obvious: of course not. He respected the way they'd gotten them, and he looked beyond.

Charlie and the other kids might not be mature enough to do that, but Lacey? Of all people, she was one of the least superficial he knew.

On the other hand, he wasn't just interested in gaining her respect. He wanted more. He wanted her to be drawn to him physically, as he was to her.

And why was he so obsessed with what Lacey thought of him, when their relationship couldn't go anywhere?

Like a slap in the face, it hit him: he was in love with her.

Not just a crush, a remnant of high school attraction.

Full-fledged, grown-up *love*.

Wow.

He just sat and tried to wrap his mind around that concept for a while, until the boys got out of the water and started throwing a football and Lacey came back toward the table.

"Hey, lazy," she said, grabbing his hand and tugging it. "The water feels great. Come get in!"

He let her pull him up and she laughed and let go of his hand, walking toward the water with a flirtatious smile over her shoulder.

All of a sudden, he didn't want to be the good friend anymore. For once, he wanted to follow his instincts and desires, to be the main man. To try and see whether his scars were really the turnoff he feared they'd be.

He pulled off his T-shirt, removed his hearing aids and located their case, all the while psyching himself up for an encounter in some ways more terrifying than heading into battle.

Chapter Twelve

Lacey's cheeks heated as she headed down toward the lake. Had she been too forward? What was she thinking, insisting that Vito come swimming?

She glanced over her shoulder to see if he was following her. When she saw him fiddling with his ear, her hand flew to her mouth.

She usually didn't even remember that he wore hearing aids. But of course, he couldn't wear them into the water.

Was that why he'd been reluctant to come in?

She glanced again. Or was it the scar

that slashed across his back, dark and very visible?

Pushing him had been a mistake. He was such a good sport he'd come if begged, but she hoped she hadn't caused him to do something he didn't want to do.

Kids shouted as they ran and splashed in the shallow part of the lake. As she walked by a group of teen girls, she inhaled the fragrance of coconut oil, something every dermatologist in the world would blanch at. Some things never changed.

She just hoped the kids and teens would be tactful about Vito's scars.

She waded into the lake, waist deep, then looked back to see whether he was following. And sucked in her breath.

The front of his chest, which she hadn't seen before, was crisscrossed with scars. Long ones and short ones, visible even with his dark Italian skin.

Their eyes met, and Vito's steps faltered a little.

Should she say something? Walk back toward him? Tell him his battle scars didn't affect her feelings toward him, except maybe to warm her heart that he'd sacrificed for his country?

But instinct told her to treat him just as she always had. Meaning, how they'd all acted at the lake as kids, since they hadn't been here together since.

He'd reached the water's edge now, and she grinned in invitation and flicked water at him with her hand. "Scared?" she taunted.

"A little." There seemed to be a double meaning in his words. "But I can play scared." He took a few steps toward her. Suddenly, he dived underwater. A few seconds later, she felt a hand wrap around her ankle, and then she was under, giggling into the green water.

She surfaced, shaking her wet hair out of her eyes. Hooked a toe around Vito's ankle and pushed hard.

He toppled backward and came up, grinning and holding up his hands. "Truce! Peace!"

Their playfulness attracted Xavier and

Charlie, who came splashing toward them. "Dad, gross—put a shirt on!" Charlie yelled loud enough for the whole beach to hear.

And apparently, despite his hearing impairment, Vito could make out the words, too.

Around them, a few kids and teens stared openly at Vito. One boy, a little older than Charlie and Xavier, said something that made the nearby kids laugh.

A flush crawled up Vito's face. "I never claimed to be a beauty queen," he said to Charlie with a half smile.

He was handling it well, but she ached for him. He'd earned those scars defending his country, and she honored him for it.

Xavier studied him thoughtfully. "Kids used to tease me for being bald, when I had cancer. Mom said to ignore them."

Vito didn't respond.

Charlie went up and tugged his arm. "Hey! Are your hearing aids out?"

Vito looked down at Charlie. "What?"

"Can't he hear?" Xavier asked.

This was getting to be a little much, and Lacey decided to intervene. "Have you boys ever heard of chicken fights?"

Neither had, so she knelt in the water and told Xavier to climb up on her shoulders. "Get on your dad's shoulders, Charlie," she said, deliberately speaking loudly. "The game is, try to knock each other off."

"Get down, Dad!" Charlie yelled into Vito's ear.

Vito grinned at her, kneeled and took Charlie onto his powerful shoulders. When he stood, he and Charlie towered over Xavier and Lacey.

"Come on, Xavier. We may be short, but we're fast," she said, and went in low.

They splashed and played for a while, with both boys getting thoroughly and repeatedly dunked. Lacey's shoulders ached from carrying a heavy, wiggling boy, but she didn't mind. The water was cool and she hadn't laughed so hard in a long time.

Most of the rest of the swimmers drifted

away, except for a few kids who talked their parents into participating.

Best of all, nobody was talking about hearing problems or scars.

Finally, Angelica called the boys to come and rest, and when she offered up watermelon as an enticement, they splashed their way to shore.

"Do you want to go get some?" Vito asked.

She shook her head. "I'm not hungry."

"Swim out to the dock?"

"Sure, and I'll beat you!" Lacey plunged her face into the water and started swimming fast.

It felt good. She seemed to have some extra energy saved up, a shaky excitement that made her want to move.

She was starting to feel such a mix of things for Vito. Admiration. Desire to protect. Caring.

Maybe even love.

She shoved that thought away and swam faster. She couldn't be falling in love with Vito, could she? Vito, her old friend and high school crush. Vito, the guy who'd always been around, always ready to lend an ear or a smile or a hand with whatever you were working on, be it figuring out algebra problems or speaking up against bullies or healing a broken heart.

Was he spending time with her now just to help her get over Gerry? It seemed like, in his eyes, she'd been seeing something more.

She reached the dock at the same moment he did, but touched it first. "I won!" she crowed into his ear.

"You did." He grinned at her as he hoisted himself out onto the wooden platform.

She found the ladder and climbed up, narrowing her eyes at him. "Wait a minute. Did you try your hardest?"

"Let's just say the D'Angelos are swimmers. And gentlemen."

"You *did* let me win!"

He didn't admit to it, but he flashed a grin that took her breath away. Standing above her dripping wet, his teeth flashing against dark skin, his eyes laughing, he looked like a hero from some ancient, epic tale.

She couldn't seem to move. She just knelt there transfixed, halfway up the ladder, staring up at him.

He extended his hand toward her. "Come aboard, milady," he said, and helped her to the dock.

She needed the help. She couldn't seem to catch her breath.

They lay side by side, faces toward the blue sky, the sun warming their wet bodies. Beside them, a little railing shielded them from those on the beach, though their shouts were still audible. Lacey was exquisitely conscious of Vito, the warmth of his arm close to hers, the even sound of his breathing.

She couldn't understand what was going on inside her. This was Vito, her old neighbor, comfortable and safe. Vito, who'd always seemed out of reach because he was older.

Yet he was someone else, too, someone

new. The things he'd been through had forged him into a man of strength and valor, a man she couldn't help but admire. It was starting to seem like she both wanted and needed him in her life.

"Do you remember coming out here as kids?" he asked unexpectedly.

"Sure." She watched a cloud laze across the sky, and then turned so she could speak into his ear. "Buck and I came with Dad pretty often when we were little."

"How come your mom never came? Was she…sick, even back then?"

"I don't know. She never wanted to do family things. Always busy with her dreams and plans, I guess."

Vito didn't answer, but he reached over and patted her hand, warm on the dock beside her.

"I don't know when she started with the pills." Lacey followed the swooping path of a dark bird, thinking about it. "I think she was okay when I was real small, but then she just started going in her bedroom and shutting the door." As she said it, she got a visceral memory of standing outside the closed door, hand raised to knock. She'd tried not to do it, knowing that Mom didn't like to be disturbed, but she hadn't been able to stop herself from knocking, then pounding on the door.

Where had Buck and her father been? Why had she been there alone for so long, with just her mother?

"If I had a kid," she said, still speaking into his ear to help him hear her, "I just hope I'd have more sense than to leave her to fend for herself like Mom did to me."

"You would. You're great with Charlie."

His automatic, assured response touched her. "Thanks, Vito."

"It's not about having the sense, it's about heart," he said with a shrug. "And heart, you've got."

His words surprised tears into her eyes. "I appreciate that."

He propped himself on one elbow to look at her, shading the sun. He was all she could see. "I can't say enough about you, Lacey. You were always sweet, and likable, and cute…"

She snorted. "Cute like a little brat, you mean."

He cocked his head to one side. "No, not exactly. I found you…appealing, as you grew up."

"You *did*?"

"Uh-huh." He reached out and brushed back a strand of her hair.

"Why didn't you ever, you know, ask me out?"

His eyebrows drew together. "You were three years younger! That wouldn't have been right."

She laughed up at him. "You're such a Boy Scout."

His eyes narrowed. "If you could read my mind, you'd know that's far from true."

"Then, or now?"

"What do you mean?"

"Are you talking about what was in your mind then, or now?" Something, some magnetic force field, drew her to reach toward his chest, the thick, luxuriant mat of hair sliced through by scars.

He caught her hand, held it still. "Don't."

"Why not?"

Shaking his head, he continued to hold her gaze.

"Because of this?" She tugged her hand away from him and traced the air above one of the multiple fault lines on his chest. Almost, but not quite, touching it.

He sucked in a breath, his eyes still pinning her. "Do you have any idea of what you're doing?"

"What am I doing?"

He caught her chin in his hand and let his thumb brush across her lower lip.

She drew in a sharp breath, staring at him. Every nerve felt alive, every sense awake.

"You have no idea how long I've wanted to do this." He leaned closer, studying her face as if trying to read her thoughts, her mood, her feelings.

"Do what?" she asked, hearing the breathy sound of her voice.

"This." He slid his hand to the back of her head and pressed his lips to hers.

The next Saturday, Vito's head was still spinning.

Kissing Lacey had been the sweetest and most promising moment of his life. Now he just had to figure out what was next.

He'd been busy with his new job for the past couple of days, and Lacey had been taking up the slack, spending extra time with Nonna and Charlie. She hadn't said anything about their kiss, but she'd given him some secret smiles that burned right into his soul.

He had to talk to her, and soon. But this morning, to give her privacy and time to get some detailed renovation work done, he'd taken Nonna and Charlie out for breakfast at the Chatterbox.

Now, seeing Charlie wave to a friend, hearing Nonna's happy conversation with a woman at a neighboring table, he felt full to the brim. His new life in Rescue River was working out, and he had a lot to be thankful for.

"Hey, Dad," Charlie said. "Am I still seeing Mom on Tuesday, now that you're working?"

"Yes. I'll drive you, and then we're going to see if the social worker can bring you home. If she can't, I can take off early." He'd explained his commitment to Charlie's schedule during his job interview, and his new employer was willing to be flexible.

"Mom said maybe she could drive me, only there's a lady she doesn't like in Rescue River."

"That's nice of her to offer, but your mom isn't allowed to transport..." All of a sudden Vito processed what Charlie had said and his heart skipped a beat. "Did she say anything about the lady?" he asked, carefully keeping his voice even.

"I think it was because of my dad. My other dad," Charlie clarified around a mouthful of pancakes. "Hey, Rafael asked if I could go to the park and play basketball, and they're leaving now. Can I?"

"Um, let me talk to his mom." His thoughts spinning, Vito slid out of the booth and made arrangements with Rafael's mother, forcing himself to focus. Charlie's social skills were improving rapidly enough that he felt okay about letting the boy go play some ball without him—after a stern warning about sportsmanship and manners.

Once that was settled, he paid the check and escorted Nonna out of the restaurant.

As they walked slowly toward the guesthouse, Vito wondered what Krystal had said to Charlie. If she was talking that openly about the past—what did it mean?

He took Nonna's arm when the sidewalk got bumpy. Quite possibly, it meant the whole truth could come out soon.

The woman in Rescue River whom Krystal had told Charlie she didn't like—and who was connected to Charlie's other dad—could be no one else but Lacey.

But Krystal didn't know Lacey, did she?

Was there a chance she'd say enough that Charlie would put it all together?

He looked over at Nonna. "What if there were something you needed to tell the truth about, only you'd made a promise not to?"

"Ah, difficult," she said, looking at him with sharp, curious brown eyes.

Clearly she was waiting for him to say more, but he didn't. If he was going to tell the truth, it had to start with Lacey. So he focused on watching a couple strapping twin babies into a double stroller.

A pang of envy swept through him. He wanted what they seemed to have. A happy, uncomplicated relationship of raising children together.

"Have you prayed about this problem?" Nonna asked.

Had he prayed? He nodded slowly. He'd sent up some urgent, brief pleas to God, for sure.

"And listened to the response?"

He blew out a breath. "Not really. I guess I need to."

They reached the guesthouse in time to see Lacey hauling a big load of trash to the curb, struggling a little. Vito jogged over and took the boxes out of her hands, earning a smile.

Lacey went to Nonna. "Are you going around the block another time? I can walk with you if Vito's got things to do." Lacey didn't look at him, but her cheeks were pink and he didn't think it was just the exertion. There had been a tentative, sweet promise in their interactions since their kiss earlier this week.

Nonna put a hand on Lacey's arm and another on Vito's. "I've had enough for now. Why don't you two walk?" She gave Vito a meaningful look, and when Lacey turned away, she mouthed *"Tell her!"*

How had Nonna guessed that his secret had to do with Lacey?

Was he supposed to tell her *now*?

As soon as they'd gotten Nonna settled on the porch with her latest large-print library book, Vito and Lacey headed out, strolling toward the park. Behind them, Wolfie barked a request to go along.

"Should we go back and get him?" Lacey asked, clearly unaware of Vito's inner turmoil. "He's about to break through the fence again."

"Not this time. I put another nail in it yesterday."

"Thanks. I'll have to get somebody to do a real repair soon." Lacey lifted her face to the sun. "I've been inside all morning, painting woodwork. The fresh air smells good."

"I'm glad you could come." He wanted to put his arm around her. He wanted to build a family with her! But the wretched secret stood between them.

Should loyalty outweigh love? He pondered the question, watching a jogger and his golden Lab loping across the park.

"We haven't had a chance to talk since you started your new job," Lacey said. "How'd it go, really? Did the kids give you a hard time?"

The cowardly side of him was grateful for

the distraction. This was territory he could handle. "It went well. The kids are a challenge, for sure, but I liked working with them."

"And your scars didn't make one bit of difference, did they?" She was smiling smugly, obviously sure she was right.

And she *was* right. "The kids made a couple of comments, but it was no big deal. I didn't overreact and the whole discussion just went away." He hesitated, then added, "You've helped me feel okay with how I look, especially because of...of how you responded to me the other day, at the lake."

She stared down at the sidewalk, but the corner of her mouth curved up in a smile.

He needed to tell her the truth about Charlie. He was going to tell her.

"I admire your being able to handle a big group of kids like that," she murmured, so quietly he had to lean down to hear her.

Thinking about how he could break the truth gently, he gave a distracted answer to her comment. "I like big groups of kids. In fact, that's my dream—to have enough kids of my own to form a baseball team."

He was about to add "with you" when she stopped still. The smile was gone from her face.

"You know what," she said, "I just realized I left something cooking on the stove. I need to run back and get it. You keep walking, okay? I don't want to interrupt your morning exercise."

She turned and hurried back toward the guesthouse.

Vito looked after her, puzzled by her abrupt departure. His *morning exercise*? And he was surprised to learn she had something cooking when she'd been painting woodwork.

He'd been about to tell her the truth. Was that God, letting him know it wasn't the right time yet?

And if so, why had Lacey suddenly started acting so weird?

Chapter Thirteen

Numb from Vito's comment about wanting a large family, Lacey stirred canned soup on the stove and tried not to think.

If she didn't think, maybe it wouldn't hurt so much that she could never, ever give Vito what he wanted.

"Miss Lacey! Miss Lacey!" Charlie barged through the screen door, letting it bang behind him. He threw his arms around her. "Guess how many baskets I made today in one-on-one?"

She clung to him for a minute, relishing the feel of sweaty boy, and then resolutely untangled herself from his arms and stepped back. Charlie was getting way too close to her, given that she'd just learned she and Vito should never, *could* never, be a couple.

"Maybe you and Dad can come watch me play," he continued, unaware of her turmoil. "And Dad said sometime we could go see a real live Cavaliers game, all three of us!"

There is no "us."

She needed to be truthful. That was kinder in the long run.

Wolfie whined at the back door and Lacey let him in, figuring the dog could comfort Charlie in the face of what she was about to say. "I don't think that's going to happen," she said, crossing her arms, deliberately keeping her distance. "You and your dad are going to move out soon, and then we won't all see so much of each other."

Charlie visibly deflated, sinking down to put his arms around Wolfie's neck. "But I don't want to move."

How quickly he accepted the truth of what she said, and her heart broke for this child who'd seen too much change and loss. She didn't know much about Charlie's background, but she knew his mom wasn't reliable enough to raise him. That had to hurt him right at the core.

And it meant he shouldn't get overly close to Lacey, because she was just going to be another loss. "You and your dad are going to be a forever family," she said, resisting the urge to hug him. "But that's not going to happen here." She forced herself to add, "It's not going to happen with me."

He looked at her with wide, sad eyes and she felt like she'd kicked a puppy. And even if her words had been for Charlie's own good, she hated that she was hurting him.

"Later," he said, then turned and straightened his shoulders. "Come on, Wolfie." And then both dog and boy ran up the stairs.

Tears rose in Lacey's eyes, and one spilled over and ran down her cheek. She wanted to call him back, to hug him and tell him that yes, they'd still be close, and yes, they could do things together in the future.

But that would just prolong the pain. Vito

needed someone who could give him and Charlie a family, and he *would* find someone.

And that someone wouldn't be her.

Automatically, for comfort, she felt for her necklace. But she wasn't wearing it. After kissing Vito, she'd decided that it was time to remove it. Time to stop focusing on Gerry, and start focusing on life ahead.

She'd been wrong.

She turned off the soup, for which she had no appetite, and trudged up the stairs. Went into her room, opened her old jewelry box and pulled the chain back out.

She'd thought she was going to make new memories with Vito and Charlie, but she was going to have to stick with the old memories. Of Gerry and the child she'd lost. Memories that didn't seem like nearly enough to build a life on now that she'd tasted what love and family could mean at Vito's side.

But Vito wanted a big family. He'd be wonderful with a big family, and she wasn't going to deny him that.

The chain and ring settling around her neck felt heavy in a way they never had before.

Suddenly bereft of energy, she closed her bedroom door, pulled the shades and lay down in the semidarkness, too tired and miserable even to pray.

Saturday afternoon, Vito arrived at the church food distribution late and out of sorts.

Lacey had been scheduled to volunteer, too, he was sure of it; she'd come out onto the porch, car keys in hand.

But when she'd realized that he and Charlie were planning to go, she'd turned abruptly and gone back inside, shutting her door with a decisive click.

Not only that, but Charlie was on his worst behavior. After Lacey's defection he'd refused to go and, when Vito had insisted, he'd let loose with a tantrum that had surely roused the neighborhood. Now he wore a sneer better befitting a teenage delinquent than an eight-year-old boy.

"Hey, Charlie's here!" Angelica waved from where she and Troy were sorting out boxes of doughnuts and pastries. "C'mon, the Kennel Kids scored the best place on the line. We get to give out the desserts, and eat whatever's left over!"

Charlie scowled, but he walked down to the end of the line where several other boys from the group stood joking and roughhousing. Troy and Angelica seemed to have them under control, though, and Xavier greeted Charlie enthusiastically.

Relieved, Vito scouted around for a role that didn't involve a lot of chitchat. He wasn't in the mood today. As the line of food bank patrons entered the church's fellowship hall and picked up boxes to fill, Vito started carrying crates of produce from the loading dock at the back of the building to resupply those on the front lines.

He tried to distract himself from his gloomy thoughts by focusing on the scent of sun-ripened tomatoes and bundles of green onions, but it didn't work. He kept going back to Lacey's pale, strained face, to the definitive click of her door closing.

Had their new connectedness been an illusion? Had she had second thoughts about pursuing a relationship with someone who had disabilities and a challenging child to raise?

Was there some way she could have found out the truth about Charlie?

But they'd walked together this morning, and she'd been perfectly fine, seeming interested in him, his job, their conversation.

"Hey, Vito!" The father of the migrant family who was renting Nonna's house—was his name Vasquez?—took the empty crate Vito handed him and started filling it with bundles of kale. "Thanks for working today."

"Thank *you*." Vito tried for a good humor he didn't feel. "I'm impressed that you're helping, as busy as you must be with the new baby."

"The bambino has not arrived yet, and my wife, she is very uncomfortable." The man worked deftly as he spoke, lining up the bundles for maximum space in the box. "She cannot work now, so I will have to join the food line this month. But at least I can help others, too."

"Good plan." Vito took the crate from Mr. Vasquez and reminded himself that his weren't the worst problems in the world. Some families struggled to scrape together enough food to eat.

He walked back toward the line, focusing on the friendly chatter between helpers and recipients. Interesting that the line between the two sometimes blurred, as with Mr. Vasquez.

He'd just put the crate down when a highly irate voice sounded behind him. "Vito! I need to talk to you!"

It was Susan Hinton, and she tugged him over toward a quiet corner of the fellowship hall. "What did you say to Lacey?"

"What do you mean?"

Susan's hands were on her hips. "She's been doing so well, but when I stopped by the guesthouse to pick her up for volunteering, she looked awful. Said she couldn't come, and when I asked her if she was sick, if she needed anything, she said no and went back in her room. She *never* misses."

Vito lifted his hands, palms up. "I could ask you the same question. She's backed off from me, just today, and I don't know why."

Susan's eyes narrowed. "Since when? What went on?"

"I have no idea."

She actually smacked him on the arm. "Come on. Don't be a typical guy. What did you say to her?"

"I don't know." He leaned against a stack of boxes, trying to recreate the scene of their walk this morning in his mind. "I was talking about my new job. And not just because I was going on and on about myself. She wanted to know. She was fine one minute, and then boom, she lit out of there like I'd insulted her best friend."

"What, exactly, did you say?" Susan leaned back, crossing her arms over her chest. "And

I'm not just being nosy. Lacey's had a lot happen to her, and she went through a pretty bad depression. I'd hate to see her sink back into that."

"Me, too." He frowned, thinking. "I was talking about working with the kids, and she said she didn't know how I could handle working with that many. I told her I love kids, want to have a passel of them myself someday, and it was about then that she seemed to back off. Was that…do you think I somehow offended her?"

Susan threw her hands up and snorted with disgust. "Vito!" Several people turned to look at them, and she tugged him closer and lowered her voice. "Look, I don't know that it's my place to tell you this, but Lacey *can't* have kids."

That hit him like a blow to deflect, news that had to be wrong. "But…she got pregnant with Gerry, right?"

She looked from one side to the other, making sure they weren't overheard. "When she miscarried, there was some damage. She's infertile now, and that's been really, really hard for her to deal with."

Pain sliced through him just as if it were he, himself, who couldn't have kids. Lacey would be such a great mom. Sometimes, life just wasn't fair.

"And so when you said..." Susan trailed off.

Understanding broke through. "Did she back off because I said I wanted a lot of kids?"

"I don't know. She's the type who'd sacrifice her own desires so other people would get what they wanted."

"Wait a minute, I'm confused. What *are* her own desires?"

"She really likes you, Vito, if you haven't wrecked it. Talk to her. That is, unless her infertility means you aren't interested in her, like some ancient king who only likes women so he can get a son."

Vito lifted his hands, palms up. "Whoa.

That's not me. Not at all." His mind was reeling, but this was something he could maybe fix. "Look, I have to go. Can you tell them... Do you think they can handle the rest without..."

"Go." Susan actually shoved him toward the door. "The line's short today and it's almost done."

"Thanks. Thanks, Susan. Let me get Charlie, and I'm outta here."

Despite the sad news he'd learned about Lacey, hope was rising in him. If she cared for him so much that she'd sacrifice her own desires so he could have kids... But didn't she see that what he wanted was her? Kids came into families in all kinds of ways. Just look at Charlie.

The boy wasn't with the rest of the Kennel Kids. "He said he needed to talk to you," Angelica said. "Didn't he come over?"

"No..." Vito turned and scanned the room. "I'll find him. Thanks."

Alongside his excitement about possibly

working things out with Lacey, self-blame pushed at him. He'd been paying so much attention to Susan's story that he'd forgotten to keep an eye on Charlie.

Finally, he thought to talk to the other Kennel Kids. "He said he was outta here, going home," one of the younger ones finally volunteered.

"Thanks." Vito blew out a breath, quickly left the church and walked the three blocks to the guesthouse at record speed. He'd told Charlie he had to stay and help the whole time. What did this new wave of defiance mean?

Nonna was at the front gate, headed out for lunch with Lou Ann Miller. "Did you see Charlie come in?" Vito asked.

"No, but I've been getting ready. I wouldn't have heard him if he went right upstairs. Is anything wrong?"

"Everything's fine. He's just in trouble."

"Don't be too hard on him, dear." Nonna

patted Vito's arm, and then the two women headed down the sidewalk.

He trotted up the stairs. Noticed the door to Lacey's room was still closed. Was she in there?

He *really* wanted to talk to her, but he had to deal with Charlie's disobedience first. He pounded on the door to Charlie's room, and when there was no answer, flung it open.

The lecture he'd been about to give died on his lips.

The room was empty. Not just empty of people, but empty of stuff. Charlie's stuff.

He opened the closet door. There was a hamper of dirty clothes, but the clean ones were gone. As was Charlie's suitcase.

His heart pounding, he ran out onto the landing. "Charlie! Charlie!"

No answer, but Lacey's door opened. "What's wrong?"

He looked from window to window, searching the yard on both sides of the guesthouse, but they were quiet, empty.

"Vito? What's going on?"

"Have you seen Charlie?"

"Not since you guys left for the church. Where is he?"

"That," Vito said grimly, "is the million-dollar question. I think he's run away."

Chapter Fourteen

Vito continued searching even as he explained the situation to Lacey, trying to stay calm.

"I just can't believe he'd run away. He's so happy here, and with you." Lacey walked into Charlie's room. She opened the closet door, and then squatted to look under the bed—all places Vito had already checked.

Vito strode into his adjoining room. He flung open the closet door and checked it top to bottom. "I never thought of him running, either, but he's not here. And his suitcase is gone." Quickly and methodically, he searched the rest of his room. News stories of all the bad things that could happen to kids played through his head, one after another.

A thought struck him and he went back to the window, lifted the screen and leaned out. He gave a whistle, and Wolfie trotted over to that side of the yard, panting, looking up expectantly.

"It's okay, boy," he said, and shut the window. Surely Charlie wouldn't have left without his beloved dog.

When he looked back into the room, Lacey was at Charlie's little desk, rifling through papers and magazines and empty potato chip bags.

"I'd better call Dion." He had his phone out to punch in the police chief's number when Lacey cried out softly.

"Look at this. Is this his handwriting?"

Vito took the torn piece of notebook paper from her and scanned it quickly, his heart sinking with every word he read.

I thot I cud have a mom and dad. I need a mom. Take care of Wofie.

And he'd signed it, "Love, Charlie."

Vito's heart seemed to stop in his chest.

"What does it mean?" Lacey clutched her arms around herself. "'I need a mom.' And who did he think would be his mom? Was it…was it me?"

"Maybe." He caught Lacey's eye, held it. "Believe me when I say I didn't try to plant that idea. But right now I'm more worried about where he's headed."

"Could he have gone to his mom?"

"That's what I'm afraid of." He turned toward the door. "I can't even imagine how upset he was, to leave without Wolfie."

"But you said she's an addict…"

"She is, and she isn't very selective about her boyfriends. I've got to find him." He headed down the stairs.

She followed behind. "Where does she live? Where has he been meeting her?"

"He's been meeting her at a center in Raystown. But she actually lives in Barnsdale. Way too far to walk, and he knows that."

Lacey grabbed his arm, stopping him. "There's a bus that goes to Barnsdale. We were talking one day, Charlie and Nonna and me, and we looked over the bus route together. He was sounding out the words, and when he came to Barnsdale, he said that's where he used to live."

Vito groaned. "I have a feeling that's exactly what he did. Is the bus stop still at the front of Cramer's Drugstore?"

She nodded. "Let's go. Maybe we can catch him before he gets the bus. I don't even know the schedule anymore, but the bus can't run very often."

They each grabbed phones, wallets and keys and rushed out to Vito's car. As they climbed in, Wolfie howled his distress at being left behind.

"Let's drive slow and watch. He could be headed back home. I doubt a bus driver would even take a kid as young as Charlie."

"I don't know. He can be pretty smart

about figuring out ways to do things and making up stories."

They were at the drugstore in minutes, and Lacey got out of the car and rushed in before Vito even had a chance to park. By the time he got inside, seconds later, she was in heated conversation with a teenage clerk.

"Why didn't anyone stop him?" she was lamenting. "A little boy, alone?"

"Kids eight and over can ride unaccompanied." The young woman shrugged. "He had the right paperwork, looked like. The driver always checks."

Vito's heart sank. Charlie was perfectly capable of talking an adult into filling out a form for him. "How long ago did the bus leave?"

The teenager looked at the wall behind her, taking what seemed like an extremely long time to skim over a schedule. "Must've been about…an hour ago?"

He and Lacey looked at each other. "Let's go," she said.

As they reached the truck, the ramifications of what might be in front of them rushed into Vito's mind. Krystal, Lacey, Charlie. All together. "Lace…you might not want to go along. Someone should stay back at the guesthouse, in case he comes back."

"I'll call Lou Ann on the way and ask her and Nonna to go back."

"It's not safe—"

"*Charlie's* not safe. And you need backup."

He pulled out of the parking lot and headed toward Barnsdale. "I need backup I don't have to worry about. You can only come if you stay in the truck and be ready to call the police if needed. That's it, Lacey. I don't want you tangling with Krystal and her boyfriends, or whoever else is crashing at her place."

"Fine."

As they drove in silence, Vito's mind hop-scotched from topic to topic. How would Charlie get from the bus stop to his house on the poorer side of town? Should he explain the whole situation about Charlie and Krystal and Gerry so that Lacey could be prepared? Why had Charlie run away, really?

He heard a small sound from the seat beside him. When he glanced over, he saw Lacey brushing her forefinger under her eye. "What's wrong?"

"I think I know why Charlie ran away," she said with a hitch in her voice. "I think it's my fault."

"How could it be your fault?" He kept his eyes on the rural road before him, pushing the speed limit.

"Because I told him we couldn't keep doing things together." She fumbled in her purse, found a tissue and blew her nose. "I told him we couldn't be a family."

Whoa. "How did you get into that conversation? When?"

"Just this morning." She paused, took a breath. "He came in from basketball, talking about all the things we three were going to do together, and I thought... I thought he'd better not expect that. So I just...told him it wasn't happening."

"Why?"

"Because it can't." He could barely hear her voice, low and hoarse.

He risked taking a hand off the steering wheel and gave her arm a quick squeeze. "We have to talk. Susan told me some stuff."

"What stuff?" She shifted to face him, sounding uneasy.

A passing road sign told Vito they were halfway to Barnsdale. "Look, I'm sorry if this is none of my business, but apparently Susan thought I should know about your infertility."

She drew in a little gasp, her hand rising to her mouth.

There was probably a tactful way to have this conversation, but he didn't know it, not now. "I'm sorry, hon. That's got to be tough, maybe the toughest thing for a woman."

She didn't say anything, and when he glanced over, her lips were pressed tightly together and her body rigid.

"But there are all kinds of ways to be a

parent. It's not just biological. I mean, look at me and Charlie."

She didn't answer, and they rode without talking into Barnsdale, passing the automobile factory on one side of the road and a couple of small machine shops on the other.

He tried again. "When all this is over, when we find Charlie and get him home safe, I want to have more of a conversation about this. Okay?"

She nodded, reached over and squeezed his arm. "We'll find him."

Vito pulled onto the street where Krystal had been renting a place, the last address he had for her. Dingy cottages and overgrown yards lined both sides of the street. "This isn't going to be pleasant. Remember, I want you to stay in the car."

"I know. I'm ready to call the cops." She looked around uneasily.

He stopped the truck in front of Krystal's place. "And Lace…"

"What?"

He hooked an arm around her neck, pulled

her to him and gave her a fast, hard kiss. Then he pulled back to look into her eyes. "Remember, whatever happens, I want this with you." He got out of the truck before he could say too much.

There was a bang as the screen door flew open and back on broken hinges, slamming into the front of the house.

"Hey, what's going on, my man Vito!" Krystal came out on the front stoop, started down the concrete steps, and then grabbed the railing and sat down abruptly.

A man appeared in the doorway behind her, the same one Vito had seen driving the SUV. The balding, bearded one who'd made Charlie cringe.

Vito strode up the narrow walkway. "Is Charlie here?"

"Yeah, he's here." Krystal held up a can of beer like she was making a toast. "Decided he'd rather live with his good old mom after all."

Relief that he'd found Charlie warred with

worry about the situation the boy had gotten himself into. "I'd like to talk to him."

The bearded man came out onto the stoop, his face unfriendly. "What's your business here?"

"Just looking for my son." Vito visually searched the place, glancing around the weedy yard, up at the little house's windows.

A curtain moved in one. Was it Charlie?

"You been stepping out on me?" The man nudged Krystal with his knee, none too gently.

"Aw, cut it out, Manny."

"You've got it wrong." Vito kept his voice calm, because he could tell that the man was volatile. "I'm just an acquaintance of Krystal's. Taking care of her son."

"You the daddy?" Manny asked.

Behind him, Vito heard the window of his truck being lowered. Lacey.

"I'm not his dad yet, but I'm going to adopt him. Let's just get him down here and I'll be on my way."

"Maybe I don't like the way you look." Manny shoved past Krystal and came down the steps. "Maybe I want you to leave right now."

Vito automatically straightened up, his fists clenching. He wanted to punch the jerk, but for Charlie's sake he couldn't. He needed to stay calm and keep things peaceful. "I'd be glad to leave you people to your own business as soon as I have Charlie."

Then everything happened at once.

Manny drew back a fist, but Krystal rushed up and grabbed it. Manny shook her off and shoved her back, roughly, causing her to fall back onto the steps. At the same moment Charlie came running out of the house. He crashed into his mother, who reached out reflexively to grab him.

Manny, unaware what was going on behind him, threw a punch that Vito dodged, but landed a second one on Vito's shoulder, knocking him back.

Behind him, the truck door opened. "Charlie!" Lacey cried. "Over here!"

Manny advanced on Vito, and with no time to regret the violence, Vito threw a one-two punch, connecting with Manny's ribs and then the side of his throat. Manny fell to the ground, gasping for air.

Vito spun to help Charlie just in time to see the boy extract himself from his mother's grip and run to Lacey. She was turning to usher him into the truck when Krystal spoke up.

"Hey!" she called, her voice slurred but plenty loud. "Wait a minute. I know who you are!"

Vito's heart skipped a beat and he ran toward Lacey and Charlie, intent on getting them into the truck so they didn't find out the truth this way.

Her heart pumping, her adrenaline high, Lacey ushered Charlie into the backseat. Then she turned to see where Vito was. She'd drive Charlie away herself if she needed to, even if it meant temporarily leaving Vito behind. He could fend for himself better than Charlie could.

Vito was approaching the truck at a run, so Lacey went around to get in the passenger's seat.

The dark-haired woman, Charlie's mother, reached the truck just as Lacey opened the passenger door. "I know who you are," she said, her tone angry.

Vito came back around from the driver's side. "Come on, Krystal, we'll talk another time. When you're sober."

"I'm sober enough to recognize *her.*"

Lacey studied the woman. "How do you know me? I don't think I've met you."

"Krystal—" Vito started.

She held up a hand and interrupted him, still glaring at Lacey. "*You're* the woman who stole my man away."

That was so far from anything Lacey expected that she could only stare at Krystal.

"Hey, now," Vito said, "this can wait. Charlie doesn't need to hear this."

Lacey stepped away from the truck door.

Before she could close it in an effort to block Charlie's hearing them, Krystal slammed it shut.

Someone clicked the locks. Vito.

She looked past Vito to Krystal, filled with a sinking feeling she didn't understand. "How do you know me?"

"Guy named Gerry McPherson sound familiar?"

"Ye-e-e-s," Lacey said slowly. "He was my husband."

"Well, he was *my* fiancé. And the father of my child."

"The father of your..."

"Him." Krystal pointed toward the backseat. "Charlie."

Lacey looked at Vito, who should be denying what this madwoman said, but Vito's face was a stone.

The edges of her world started to crumble. "Gerry was Charlie's father?"

"That's right. I gave him more than you ever did."

The words stabbed her, but she ignored

the pain. She had to explain to the woman how wrong she was. "But Charlie's eight. I was married to Gerry when…" She stared at Krystal.

Krystal threw up her hands. "You didn't even know, did you?"

Slowly Lacey shook her head. What she was hearing couldn't possibly be right.

"Yeah, he was seeing me on the side. At first, I didn't know about you, either." The anger was draining out of the woman's voice. "When I figured out that he was married, I tried to break it off, but he said your marriage was on the rocks and he was leaving. It was only when I saw that photo in the paper that I realized he'd been lying. You two were hugging each other like lovebirds, all happy." She shook her head, her expression bitter. "He wasn't worth the time I put into him."

"At least you got… Charlie." She heard the choked sound of her own voice as if from a distance.

Gerry had been cheating on her?

Could it be true?

She cleared her throat. "How long were you seeing him?"

"Couple of years. He didn't come around as much after Charlie was born. To be fair, he was overseas a lot after that."

"Don't be fair to him!" Lacey snapped. "Did he see you when he came home, too?"

"Yeah. Some. Not much." Something like compassion had crept into Krystal's voice. "Charlie doesn't remember him."

Lacey sagged back against the truck, unable to process what she was hearing.

Gerry had been unfaithful during the whole course of their marriage.

He'd conceived a son with this woman in front of her.

He'd met the son and seen the woman when he came home on leave.

And she'd known none of it.

She put her hands over her face, trying to block it out, trying to preserve the memory of the husband she'd adored, of the happy marriage she'd thought she had.

Vito cleared his throat.

The sound brought a whole new betrayal into focus, and she dropped her hands away from her eyes and turned to stare at him. "You knew."

Slowly, he nodded.

"You knew, and you stayed in my house, brought Gerry's son into my house, and you didn't tell me."

"Cold, Vito," Krystal said.

"Lacey, I wanted to tell you. Started to, so many times. But I promised Gerry I wouldn't."

Krystal snorted. "Yeah, well, we all made promises, didn't we? And look how much good that did."

Lacey stared from Krystal to Vito, trying to process it all.

Vito was still talking. "I promised that I'd take care of Charlie and look out for you, too. He knew how much it would hurt you…"

"Oh, that's rich," Krystal said.

Lacey just stared and shook her head. He'd kept the truth from her so as not to *hurt* her? At Gerry's behest?

There was a sound from inside the truck, and she turned to see Charlie knocking on the window and mouthing words, his face anxious.

Lacey just stared at him, the boy she'd come to care for so much. The boy whose eyebrows arched high and dark, just like Gerry's had.

He was Gerry's son.

Gerry *had* a son. She herself had had so much trouble conceiving, and when she'd finally gotten pregnant, it had been too late: Gerry had been killed, and she had lost the baby.

Charlie was rattling the truck door now, and Vito and Krystal were arguing about something, but the words blurred into a mishmash she couldn't understand.

It was all too much. She had to get out of here.

She spun away and started walking down the road, faster and faster until she was nearly at a run.

Chapter Fifteen

For a few seconds, Vito was paralyzed, watching Lacey disappear down the street.

Charlie's rattling of the door and the sounds of Krystal's voice speaking to Manny, who was waking up, snapped him out of it.

He needed to go after Lacey. He needed to reassure and help Charlie. And he probably needed to make sure Krystal was okay, too.

The confusion of prioritizing made his military training kick in. *Secure those closest and most vulnerable.*

He opened the truck door and leaned in toward Charlie. "Listen, we're going to talk this through and figure it all out."

Charlie slumped. "Am I in trouble?"

"Yes, you're in trouble, but everyone gets in trouble. It's okay." He knew what Charlie would ask next, and he held up a hand to forestall it. "You're not getting sent away. You're still going to be my son and you can still see your mom every week."

"What about Miss Lacey?"

Vito blew out a breath. No dishonesty. That was what had gotten him in trouble in the first place. "I just don't know, Charlie. She's pretty mad at me right now."

"How come?"

"Grown-up business. We'll talk about it later." He stood, patted Charlie's shoulder, and then reached in and gave the boy a hug. "Sit tight. I've got to check on your mom and then we'll go make sure Lacey is safe."

He shut Charlie's door gently, and then walked a few steps toward Krystal. "You going to be okay?" he asked, nodding toward Manny. "I can call the cops for you."

"I got this," she said. "Go after her."

He took her word for it and drove out in

the direction Lacey had gone, scanning the road. It was late afternoon and clouds were rolling in, thick and ominous. He had to get her before this storm started—or, given the neighborhood, something worse happened. "Help me watch for Lacey," he told Charlie.

A moment later, Charlie leaned forward in the seat and pointed. "Is that her?"

He could see her yellow shirt. She was desperately waving down a truck. No. She wouldn't get in a stranger's vehicle. Would she?

Did she want to avoid him that badly?

The truck stopped. The passenger door opened, and Lacey climbed in.

Vito hit the gas. "Do you know anyone who drives a blue pickup?" It seemed to have writing on the side, but Vito couldn't read it.

His stomach was lurching. If something happened to Lacey...

He got behind the truck, which was traveling at a normal rate of speed, and was relieved to see it was headed toward Rescue

River, rather than away. Maybe she'd known the person and was getting a safe ride. But he still followed, just to be sure.

His head was still spinning from the way it had all gone down. Lacey had found out the truth about Gerry in the worst possible way.

Why hadn't he told her before? The betrayal in her eyes had just about killed him.

How awful for her to find out about her adored, war hero husband from his lover, screaming jealously at her.

And normally, she'd have turned to him for comfort. But instead, she'd looked at him as the betrayer, and rightly so.

Except he'd promised Gerry he wouldn't tell.

He tried to think of how it could've worked out differently. What all he'd done wrong. He shouldn't have made the promise. He shouldn't have moved in with Lacey. But that had been for Nonna…

There was a sniffle from the seat behind him, and Vito pulled his attention away from his thoughts and to Charlie. "Hey, buddy. What's the matter?"

"I thought Mom would want me," Charlie said in a subdued voice. "But when I got to her house, she told me to go away because Manny would get mad. And then Manny saw me."

"Did he hurt you?" Vito would kill the man if he had.

"No, but he made Mom shut me in the bedroom. And they said I couldn't come out. And they were gonna call you, but then they started fighting and kind of forgot about me."

"You can't do that, buddy. You can't run away. And you can't live with your mom." As he spoke, he was watching the truck in front of him, relieved to see it taking the exit that led to the guesthouse.

"I know." Charlie's voice was subdued.

"We're gonna figure this out, talk about it." Vito reached over and ruffled Charlie's hair. "Right now, though, we've got to check on Lacey."

He followed the truck, and when it pulled up in front of Lacey's place, he pulled up behind it.

"Do I have to stay in the truck again?" Charlie's voice was quiet.

"No, buddy, but you have to let me talk a little bit to Lacey. Grown-up business. Go see Wolfie. Okay? Take him out and walk him down the street, but stay where you can see me. We'll go inside in just a minute."

"Good, because I'm hungry."

They both got out of the truck, and Vito watched to make sure Charlie was safely out of earshot. He turned in time to see a dark-haired man walking beside Lacey toward the front door.

Jealousy burned inside him. He didn't want anyone else walking with Lacey. Especially not some tall, buff, thirty-ish guy with no scars and, probably, no baggage.

He followed them up the steps. "Lacey, I need to talk to you."

She ignored him and turned to the dark-haired man. "Thank you for the ride."

"Would you like me to stay?" the man asked in a courteous voice with just a trace of a Spanish accent.

She glanced toward Vito without meeting his eyes. "Maybe for a few minutes, if you don't mind. I just need to talk to…my other boarder, without him bothering me, and make a couple of arrangements."

"It's no problem." He sat down in the porch chair Vito had begun to consider his own.

Lacey turned to go inside.

Vito started to follow. "Lacey—"

"The lady prefers that you don't come in," the other man said, standing up to block Vito as Lacey continued on inside.

Vito stopped, lifted an eyebrow, wondered if he was going to have to fight again that day.

"She's an old friend, and she told me on the way home that she doesn't want you around. Not my business why." The man shrugged. "Sorry, man."

Vito sat down heavily on the front steps. He could smell someone barbecuing for Saturday dinner. He and Lacey had done the same just last week.

Before everything had fallen apart.

Charlie came back into the yard, tugging Wolfie. He started up the steps. "Let's go in. I'm starving."

"Can't. Not yet."

"Why not?"

"Lacey is… She doesn't want us to come in just yet, but we can in a little while."

Charlie's lower lip began to stick out. "I want to go to my own room."

Except it wasn't his own room. "Just a little while, buddy."

The dark-haired man stood and went down to his truck. He came back with a sandwich encased in plastic wrap and an apple. "Here," he said to Charlie. "It's good. Turkey and cheese."

"Thanks!" Charlie grabbed the sandwich and started unwrapping it.

"That's your lunch, man," Vito protested.

"I have kids. I understand." He sat back down in the same porch chair.

"Hey, you don't have to wait around. I won't bother her."

"I said I'd wait," the man said quietly. "No offense."

So they sat in silence while Charlie scarfed down the sandwich, and then played in the yard with Wolfie. It was another forty-five minutes before Lacey came out the door.

"Thanks, Eduardo," she said, still not looking at Vito. "I'm sorry to keep you from your work. I'm fine now."

"You're sure?"

"I'm sure."

They both watched as Eduardo trotted down the steps and swung into his truck. Charlie came over, holding Wolfie tight on his leash, in control for once. "Hi, Miss Lacey," he said uncertainly.

She knelt in front of him, giving Wolfie a quick head rub, and then turning her full attention to Charlie. "I need to talk to you about something serious," she said. "Can you listen?"

He nodded, eyes wide.

"I like you a lot," she said. "I'm really sorry it didn't work out for me and your dad, but that's not your fault."

Charlie swallowed hard, and Vito did the same.

"You always have a safe home with your dad. That isn't changing. You don't run away from him anymore, okay?"

"Okay." Charlie's voice was low.

"And because I really like you, this is hard, but...you and your dad are going to need to move out."

Charlie looked down at the floor, nodded and turned away, nuzzling his face in Wolfie's fur. Wolfie, seeming to understand the boy's sadness, whined a little and licked Charlie's face.

Vito felt like he'd been punched in the stomach, hard.

Lacey stood and faced him. "Vito, I've made arrangements for Nonna to stay at the Senior Towers. They have a room open for her for however long she needs, and they can help her move in tomorrow. I have a call in to a friend of mine, a nurse, who'll check on her every day."

"You didn't have to—"

"Let me finish." She held up a hand. "You're going to have to find another place for you and Charlie to stay. I'm going away for a few days, and I want you out when I get back." Her voice was cold and distant.

She didn't wait for an answer, but turned and walked into the house, letting the door bang behind her.

Vito's shoulders slumped and he felt like collapsing down onto the porch and burying his head in his hands.

She was really, truly rejecting him. He loved her, and he'd lost her. Despair clutched his stomach with strong, cold fingers.

But he had a son to care for.

He swallowed the lump in his throat and straightened his shoulders. Looked out across the lawn.

There was Charlie's basketball. They couldn't forget that.

He walked down the steps, heavily, to pick it up.

"We gonna play, Dad?" Charlie asked eagerly.

"No, son." Vito carried the basketball up the stairs, not even bouncing it. "We're going to have to start packing, and I have to start looking for a new place for us to live."

He went to the front door, held it open for Charlie, and then followed the boy inside.

He felt utterly broken. And the only reason he was standing upright, trying to be strong, was because Nonna and Charlie depended on him.

It was Lacey's fifth day at the Ohio Rural Retreat Center, and she was finding some small measure of peace.

She'd cried so much that her eyes felt permanently swollen. She'd prayed almost continually. She'd sought counsel with the center's spiritual advisors.

She knew now that she needed to put her faith in God, not men.

She knew she wasn't healed yet, not even close.

The thought of Fiona Farmingham coming to visit with her today was terrifying. It wasn't that she didn't like Fiona; she barely knew her. And she had Fiona to thank for the idea of coming here. When she'd blurted out a piece of an explanation to Eduardo in that horrible truck ride home—"my husband wasn't who I thought he was"—Eduardo had urged her to get in touch with Fiona, who'd had something similar happen to her. And then he'd gone further and called Fiona, who'd texted her the address of the retreat center where she'd stayed when her world had fallen apart.

There was a knock on the door of her small, monk-like cell. "Your visitor is here," came the quiet, soothing voice of the retreat receptionist.

Trying not to show her reluctance, Lacey

went out to the reception area and greeted Fiona with a handshake, then an awkward hug.

"Would you like to walk?" Fiona asked. "When I was here, I always liked the trail around the pond."

"Um, sure." She hoped Fiona didn't plan to stay long, that she wouldn't say anything to burst the fragile, peaceful bubble Lacey had built around herself.

But it couldn't last forever, of course. She was going to have to get back to renovating the guesthouse. To rebuilding her life in Rescue River as a strong single woman.

That had been her goal all along. When and why had she let that fade? But she knew the answer: it was when Vito and Charlie had come. Ever so gradually, they'd slipped into her heart so that now, having lost them, she didn't feel strong. She felt weak and vulnerable and raw.

"Thanks for agreeing to a visit," Fiona said as they walked toward the center's small pond, separated from the main building by a stand of trees. "I just felt really led to talk to you. And if your nights have been anything like mine were, you're not sleeping well, so I figured an early morning visit would be okay."

"I appreciate it," Lacey lied politely. "Where are your kids?"

"With the nanny," Fiona said, sounding apologetic. It was no secret that she was quite wealthy after her scandalous divorce settlement, but she didn't flaunt her money; in fact, people said she didn't like mentioning it.

A red-winged blackbird, perched on a cattail at the pond's edge, let out its trademark "okalee, okalee" before taking flight, bright red and yellow wing patches flashing in the early morning sun. "This is an amazing place," Lacey said, meaning it. "Thank you for telling me about it."

"Of course. How are you doing?" The

question wasn't a surface platitude, but a real inquiry.

"I'm…managing, but barely," Lacey admitted.

"That's normal," Fiona said matter-of-factly. "When I found out my husband had a whole other family, it took a year to even start to feel normal again."

Her blunt words reached Lacey in a way the retreat counselors' soothing tones hadn't. Fiona had been there, had experienced the loss and humiliation Lacey was going through. "Did you ever feel like it might have been a dream, like you were going to wake up any minute and none of it would be true?"

Fiona nodded. "All the time. And then you keep on realizing, no, it's true, my life wasn't at all like what it seemed to be."

"Exactly. It's like my memories were stolen. The happiness I had with Gerry was all a huge lie."

"Well." Fiona reached out to run her fingers alongside the reeds that rimmed the pond. "I don't know if it was all a lie. My therapist said that men who lead double lives can really believe they love both women. Or in my case, both families."

Lacey inhaled the rich, damp-earth fragrance of the wetlands. "I don't know how you stood it, with four kids to watch out for. I'm barely managing with just myself."

"You do what you have to do. For me, the betrayal was the worst part. It messed with my whole image of myself as a woman, like I wasn't enough."

Lacey looked over at Fiona, tall, with long, wavy red hair and an hourglass figure. *She* had felt like she wasn't enough? "Did you get over that?"

Fiona shook her head. "You will, I'm sure, but I didn't. I've got my hands full with my kids and starting a business. Even if I felt like I could trust a man again—which I don't—I wouldn't have time for it."

"I hear you. My guesthouse is yelling for me to get back to renovations."

They walked in companionable silence

for a few minutes. Green-headed mallards flew down and landed on the pond, skidding along. Overhead, the sky turned a brighter blue.

"I just wonder if everyone in town knew but me," Lacey burst out finally.

"I wondered the same thing, and I found out as soon as the truth started getting publicized. People *did* know, and they rushed to tell me how they'd suspected, or what they'd heard." She sighed. "That was bad enough, but when my kids started getting teased and bullied, I'd had it. I had to leave. It's why I moved to Rescue River."

"Oh, how awful for you *and* your kids!" Lacey felt almost ashamed for being upset about her own situation. Fiona, with her four kids suffering, had it so much worse.

"It was awful, but things are better now. Much better. What happened with your husband? How did you find out?"

So Lacey explained the whole situation. "And then Vito, he brought Gerry's child into my home! He was living there all along, knowing that secret."

"Ouch."

The sun was rising higher, and Lacey slipped off her sweatshirt and tied it around her waist. "He was an old friend, but he lied to me."

"Did he actively lie? He seems like a really nice guy, but you never know."

Lacey thought back. "No, he never actively lied. I think the subject of Charlie's dad might have come up once, but he told me Charlie's father had died. And that he was Vito's war buddy. All of which was technically true. But—" she lifted her hands, palms up "—why did he come to live in the guesthouse—with my husband's son—when he had to know how much the truth would hurt me? And then we…" Tears rose to her eyes and she blinked them back. "We started getting close. I thought he cared for me." She almost choked on her words.

Fiona put an arm around her, giving her a quick shoulder-hug. "That sounds so hurtful. But do you think he did it on purpose, to be mean?"

Unbidden, an image of Vito's kind face swam before Lacey's teary eyes. She thought back over the time when he'd decided to stay at the guesthouse. "Nooooo," she said slowly. "He was actually reluctant to stay, and only agreed because his grandma was so keen on it."

"So he didn't exactly come knocking on your door, looking for a place to live."

"No. But he should have told me the truth!"

"He should have." Fiona hesitated. "That's a pretty hard thing to tell."

"I guess." Lacey didn't want to look at Vito's side, not yet. She was still too angry at him.

"And the thing is, were you perfect? That's what my counselor made me look at, in my situation. Were there any mistakes you made, in your marriage?"

"I was stupid," Lacey said bitterly.

"Well…yeah. You kind of were."

Lacey blinked, surprised. Not many people would speak that bluntly to someone who wasn't an old friend.

"We weren't wise as serpents, were we?" Fiona stared off into the distance. "Neither of us. And people suffered because of it."

Lacey had never thought of it that way. She'd focused on how she was an innocent victim, not on how she'd had a responsibility to be wise as well as gentle and kind.

And yes, people had suffered. She thought of Charlie's hurt face when she'd told him she wouldn't be doing things with Vito anymore. It was a big part of why he'd run away.

Kicking him and Vito out on the street... Making Nonna move to the Towers... Yeah. "I've made a lot of people miserable, dragged them down with me."

They were coming to the end of the loop around the pond. "Don't beat yourself up. That's not what I mean at all. I'm really sorry for what happened to you. It's just... we're all a mix, right? Nobody's perfect. Not your husband, not you. And not Vito, either."

"True."

They walked quietly for a few more minutes, and when they reached the parking lot, Fiona stopped. "I've got to get back to the kids. But I just want you to know, there's life after this. You can come back, live well. Keep on praying, and I'll pray for you, too."

They hugged, for real this time. "Thanks for coming to see me," Lacey said. "It helped. A lot."

And as she waved, and then headed back inside, she felt better. Not healed, but better. And it was a good thing, because tomorrow she had to go back to town, hold her head high and probably encounter Vito and Charlie.

Chapter Sixteen

A week later, Vito parked in front of the Senior Towers and headed inside. He'd been so busy with Charlie and his job that he hadn't visited his grandmother for the past couple of days, and he felt guilty.

That wasn't the reason for the heaviness in his soul, though. *That* came from his unresolved issues with Lacey. Even now, if he looked down the street, he could see her on the porch of her guesthouse, talking and laughing with a couple of visitors.

He hoped to catch her eye, but she didn't even glance his way.

He trudged inside the Senior Towers, trying to look at the bright side. Charlie was doing well; Vito had explained the whole situation to his social worker, and a couple of sessions with her, Vito, and Charlie had helped the boy to understand as much of the truth as an eight-year-old needed to know. They'd talked over running away, and Charlie had promised to make a phone call to his social worker if he ever felt like doing it again.

They'd found half of a double to rent on the edge of town, with a huge fenced yard and a dog-friendly neighbor in the other half of the house. So that was another good thing.

His course work was going well, and his new job even better. He loved working with the at-risk boys, and already his supervisor had talked with him about a possible full-time opening once he had his degree.

The scars weren't really an issue, in the job or otherwise. In fact, he felt almost foolish about how much he'd let them get in his way when he'd first returned to Rescue River. Now if a newcomer stared or a kid made a comment, he could let it roll off him, knowing that to most people, it was what was inside that mattered.

Lacey had helped him see that first. He owed her a debt of gratitude, but it was one he couldn't pay. To approach her again, after what he'd done, would be an insult to her.

He straightened his shoulders and ordered himself to focus on what he could do, not on what he couldn't. He'd go spend time with Nonna, help her feel better and recover from the move.

He walked into the Senior Towers and crossed the lobby. He was about to push the button on the elevator when he distinguished Nonna's voice, and he turned to see her emerging from the exercise room in the midst of a crowd of women. She wore hot pink sweats and a T-shirt that said… He squinted and read the words, Vintage Workout Queen.

She walked to him and gave him a strong hug. "My Vito! Come on. Sit down here in the lobby. I can spare a few minutes before I meet with my business partners."

Vito blinked. "Business partners?"

"Yes, Lou Ann and Minnie. The matchmaking business is taking off. Now, tell me what's new with you, and you know what I mean."

He tried to deflect the conversation to his work, and to Charlie, but Nonna saw right through it.

"I'm glad those things are going well, but what about Lacey? Have you mended that fence yet?"

He shook his head. "No, and I don't think it's going to get mended. Some things just can't be fixed." Nonna didn't know the details of what had happened between them, didn't know about Charlie's parentage, but she knew something serious had split them apart.

"Bella? Are you ready?" It was Lou Ann Miller, and it took Vito a minute to realize she was talking to Nonna. He'd almost forgotten his grandmother had a first name. "Oh, hello, Vito."

"Go rouse Minnie," Nonna instructed the other woman. "We have to do a quick consultation with our first client, Vito, here, before we start working on our business plan."

That was the *last* thing he needed. "Nonna… I was really just coming to check on you, not to talk about my own troubles. How are you feeling?"

She waved a hand. "I'm fine. Better every day, and these ladies—" she waved toward Lou Ann and Minnie, now both coming down the hall, talking busily "—they keep me in the loop. Lou Ann knows about all the news outside the Towers, and Minnie knows what's going on inside. I love it here!"

Vito felt a pang. He wasn't really needed by his grandma, not anymore. Nonna was making a new life for herself.

The other two women reached the cozy corner where Nonna and Vito sat, and Lou Ann pulled up chairs for both of them, leaving Vito surrounded and without an escape route.

Immediately, Nonna launched an explanation. "Vito, here, is estranged from the woman he most loves, because of some kind of fight. He thinks the relationship is doomed."

"Do you still have feelings for her?" Lou Ann demanded.

He was torn between telling the three interfering woman to go jump in the lake and embracing them for taking his troubles seriously. He chose the latter. "I still have feelings. But I did something that hurt her terribly."

"Did you apologize?" Miss Minnie asked.

"Yes, of course. But she kicked me out of the guesthouse, and she isn't speaking to me."

"Why did you do it?" Lou Ann asked.

He shrugged helplessly. "Loyalty, I guess. Loyalty to an old friend."

"Loyalty is an important value," Miss

Minnie said. "But love…remember your Bible, Vito. The greatest of these is Love."

It was true. He saw that now, too late.

"So he's just backing away. Out of politeness!" Nonna leaned forward and pinched his cheek. "My Vito. Always the best friend. Always so nice."

"Too nice," Miss Minnie declared.

Lou Ann Miller looked thoughtful. "If you give up on her, maybe you just don't care enough. Why, I know a couple right here in Rescue River who had to keep huge secrets from each other. But they pushed through their problems. Now they're happily married."

Happily married. If there was any possibility at all of that for him and Lacey…

"The choice is yours," Nonna said. *"Coraggio, ragazzo mio."*

Lacey was what he wanted most in the world. Could he risk another try, a heartfelt apology, a grand gesture that might sway her back in his direction?

What did he have to lose?

Nonna seemed to see the decision on his face. "If you need any help," she said, "we're here for you."

He stood and kissed her cheek. "I will most definitely take you up on that."

From a high-backed chair that faced away from their corner, Gramps Camden stood and pointed a finger at Vito. "For once, the ladies are right. Being polite doesn't get a man much of anything."

As the ladies scolded Gramps for eavesdropping, Vito waved and headed for the door, feeling more energy with each step he took.

He had some serious planning to do.

A week later, Lacey hugged Nonna at the door to the Senior Towers, glad to feel that the older woman was gaining weight and strength. "Don't worry," she said. "I'll take you to the party next week. Are you sure you don't want me to walk you upstairs?"

"I'm fine. And I'm sorry I got the date

wrong. Maybe I'm losing my marbles." Nonna shrugged.

"It's all right. I enjoyed spending some time with you." Truthfully, the excursion had filled a gap in Lacey's week. Even though she'd tried to rebuild her life, to spend time with girlfriends and focus on her work, she still found herself lonely.

Still found herself missing Vito and Charlie.

Nonna reached up and straightened Lacey's collar, plucked a stray hair off her shoulders. "Do you know what we always said in Italy? *Si apra all'amore.* Be open to love."

"Um, sure." Maybe Nonna *was* getting a little confused, because that remark had been apropos of nothing.

She drove the half block to the guesthouse and parked in the driveway, taking her time. She didn't want to go inside an empty house. Without Charlie roughhousing and Wolfie barking, without Vito's deep voice, the place felt empty.

But delaying wouldn't solve her problem. She clasped the cross she'd hung around her neck, in place of the wedding ring she'd worn before. It was a reminder: she could do all things through Christ.

Including survive loneliness.

She climbed out of the car and walked slowly toward the front entrance, checking her flower beds, which were doing great. Looked reflexively at the broken fence. She really needed to...

She stopped. Looked again.

The makeshift fix they'd done weeks ago, when Wolfie had escaped, wasn't there. Instead, the fence was repaired.

She knelt down, awkward in her dress and heels, and examined it. The two broken pickets had been replaced with new ones, painted white. Only when you were very close could you see that the paint was a little brighter on the new pickets.

She frowned. Who would have repaired her fence?

Wondering, she walked toward the front

of the house. As she rounded the corner, she heard music.

Opera music. *Italian* opera music.

What had Nonna called it? *The most romantic music on earth.*

What in the world?

The wonderful smell of Italian food— lasagna?—wafted through the air.

As she climbed the front steps, she saw something pink.

Her heart pounding, she reached the top of the steps. A trail of rose petals led her across the porch to a table set for two, topped with a white tablecloth.

She stared at the centerpiece, and tears rose to her eyes.

A ceramic rooster, exactly like the one Charlie had broken the day she'd met him.

No longer could she doubt who was responsible for what she was seeing.

She turned toward the front door. At the same moment, Vito emerged through it, a bowl of salad in one hand and a tray of pasta in the other. He wore dress trousers, a white dress shirt and an apron. Focused on balancing both dishes, he didn't notice her at first, but when he did, a strange expression crossed his face.

"Lacey," he said his voice intent. "Wait." He turned and carefully put down the two items on a side table.

Then he undid his apron and took it off, his eyes never leaving hers.

"How did you…" She broke off.

Walking slowly across the porch, he stood before her, not touching her. "I trespassed. Nonna gave me her key."

"Nonna…" She cocked her head to one side and reviewed the afternoon. Nonna's sudden invitation to a party, her insisting that Lacey dress up, the realization that it was the wrong date… "She was in on this. And you fixed my fence."

"For a good cause."

"What do you mean?"

He walked around her and pulled out a chair. "Explaining will take a minute. Would you like to sit down?"

She hesitated, feeling a little railroaded, but curious, too. "Oka-a-a-ay."

He poured iced tea, the raspberry flavor she always ordered at the Chatterbox, looking for all the world like a handsome Italian waiter. But then he pulled a chair to face her and sat down, close enough that their knees almost touched. Almost, but not quite. "The good cause is…an apology. Lacey, I am so sorry for what I did to you. There's no excuse for dishonesty."

She wanted to forgive him instantly. The music, the tea, the rose petals, the mended fence, the ceramic rooster—all of it created a romantic little world. But she couldn't just succumb to it. She needed to be as wise as a serpent, not just gentle as a dove. Not just go with her heart. "I would like to hear why you did what you did. I wasn't in a condition to listen before."

He drew in a breath and nodded. "Of course. You deserve that." Still, he seemed reluctant to speak.

"I can take it, Vito! Whatever happened, it's probably better than what I've been imagining."

"Right." He reached for her, then pulled his hand back. "It was only in the last couple of months of Gerry's life that I found out he'd been unfaithful to you."

The word stung, even though she knew it was true. "How did you find out?"

"He was burning letters," he explained. "Building a fire was dangerous over there, so I went to stop him. He said he had just a few more to burn, and he was turning over a new leaf. I still had to stop him—I was his commanding officer by then—and I happened to see a...suggestive card. It didn't look like something you'd send, so I asked him about it."

The thought of another woman sending racy cards to her husband made Lacey's face hot with anger and humiliation. Was that what Gerry had wanted in a woman? Hadn't her tame, loving letters been enough?

Vito was watching her face, and he reached

out and wrapped his hand around her clenched fist. "He was *burning* it, Lace. He'd had a couple of risky encounters that had made him think about his life, and he wanted to get a fresh start."

"Either that, or he was afraid of getting caught."

"No, I think he was sincere. He really did love you. He just wasn't used to…" Vito seemed to cast about for the right word. "To monogamy, I guess. That's why I regret introducing you two."

"That's why you tried to warn me about him. You knew what he was like."

Vito nodded. "But you were in love, and I hoped marriage would change him. And it did. It just took a while. When you let him know you were expecting a baby, it made him want to change his ways, be a better husband and father."

"He already had a child!"

"Yeah." Vito sighed. "I found out about that at the very end. You sure you want to hear?"

"Tell me."

"Okay." He looked out toward the street, his shoulders unconsciously straightening into military posture. "Three of us were cut off from the others, and both Gerry and Luiz were hit and bleeding pretty bad. When Luiz died and Gerry realized the medics might not get there in time for him, either, he told me about Charlie. He asked me to take care of Charlie if Krystal couldn't. And he asked me to look out for you, and to keep you in the dark about who Charlie was, because he thought it would kill you to know. Before I could make him see it wasn't possible to do all those things together, he was gone."

Lacey just sat, trying to process what Vito was saying.

"I tried to save him, Lace. And I tried to do what he asked, though I didn't succeed very well." He sighed. "I thought things were okay for Charlie and Krystal. I thought it might be best for you if I stayed away. But then I got injured, and there was the rehab, and then everything hit the fan with Krystal and I found out Charlie was about to be put into the system… Well, first things first, I thought. Charlie is a kid."

"Of course." Lacey stared down at the porch floor. "It was my own fault I was so foolish, marrying Gerry. I was vulnerable to anyone."

"I was foolish, too, but I've learned. I've learned that honesty and…and *love*…trump loyalty to a bad cause."

She froze, not daring to look at him. "Love?"

He squeezed her hand, then reached up to brush a finger across her cheek. When he spoke, his voice was serious. "I love you, Lacey. I… Maybe I always have, kind of, but now it's grown-up and serious and forever."

Cautiously she looked at him through her eyelashes, not wanting to let her joy and terror show. She drew in a breath. "I have an apology to make, too. I was wrong to kick you and Charlie out. I was angry at Gerry, really, and at myself, and I took it out on you."

"Understandable."

"Is Charlie okay?"

He nodded. "We've had a few sessions with his social worker to talk it all through. She helped me understand how much to tell Charlie. Right now, he knows that his dad was a hero, but made some mistakes. That he felt ashamed he wasn't married to Charlie's mom. And that none of it is Charlie's fault. That seems like about as much as he can take in, right now."

"That's good." She bit her lip. "I shouldn't have taken out my hurt on you, and especially on an innocent child."

"For whatever you did wrong, I forgive you."

"And I forgive you."

They looked at each other. "Are we good?" he asked.

"We're good." She felt a strange breathlessness as he stood and pulled her gently to her feet.

And into his arms.

Being held by him, seeing and believing how much he cared, soothed some deep place inside her that wanted to be cared for and loved.

His hand rubbed slow circles on her back. "I hated being at odds," he said, and she felt the rumble of his voice against her cheek. "I want to be your friend. At *least* your friend. I want to be more."

She pulled away enough that she could look up at his face. "What kind of more?" she murmured in a husky tone that didn't even sound like her.

"This kind." He leaned down and pressed his lips to hers.

After a long while he lifted his head, sniffing the air, and then pulled away.

Lacey smelled it at the same time he did. "Something's burning!"

They ran inside and Vito pulled a scorched cake from the oven. "Oh, man, it was chocolate, too!"

She burst out laughing.

And then they were both laughing, and crying, and hugging each other, and kissing a little more. "It was so awful being apart from you. I never want that to happen again," he said.

"I don't, either." She pulled back. "But Vito. That nice meal is getting cold."

He laughed. "It'll warm up just fine. Come here."

He was right, of course. She stepped forward into his arms. "I love you," she said.

Epilogue

One Year Later

"I predicted this as soon as I saw you catch that bouquet," Susan Hinton said, looking around the guesthouse lawn with satisfaction.

"You couldn't have!" Lacey laughed. "Vito wasn't even back yet."

"I saw him come up behind you and I knew."

Gina, Lacey's sister-in-law, came over to where Lacey and Susan sat, under the party tent they'd put up against a summer shower. "Vito and Buck are exchanging fatherhood tips with Sam."

Lacey craned her neck and saw Sam Hinton, holding three-month-old Sam Jr. as if he were made of glass. Buck squatted to wipe the cake from little Bobby's face. And Vito was bending down to speak to Charlie, who looked adorably grown-up in his junior tux.

Lacey felt fully recovered from the devastating news about Gerry being Charlie's father. There even seemed to be a strange rightness in her helping Vito to raise Gerry's child.

Nonna approached Vito and took his arm, pulling him toward Lacey. She seemed years younger than she had after her heart attack; indeed, she was helping to teach heart attack recovery classes at the Senior Towers and was so happily enmeshed in the social circles there that she'd decided to live at the towers full-time.

"I need to talk to the bride and groom," Nonna said as she reached Lacey and her friends. "Alone."

Vito lifted an eyebrow and reached to pull Lacey from her reclining position. The very touch of his hand gave her goose bumps. They'd spent glorious time together during the past year, getting to know each other as the adults they were now. Vito had finished his online studies and student teaching, and had the offer of a job for the fall. Meanwhile, he'd been working with Lacey at the guesthouse, which had become so successful that she'd had to hire help—help that would now manage the place while she and Vito honeymooned.

The thought of their honeymoon on a South Carolina beach made Lacey's skin warm. She couldn't even regret that they could only manage a long weekend, with the guesthouse to run and Charlie to parent. She was so, so ready to begin married life with Vito.

"I'm afraid I've been interfering again," Nonna said, a twinkle in her eye.

"Nonna! What now?" Vito's tone was indulgent.

"You have that look on your face," Lacey added. "What have you been up to?"

Nonna looked from Vito to Lacey and bit her lip. "First, I have a confession to make." She hesitated, then added, "My interfering has been going on for a while."

"What do you mean? The matchmaking date?" Lacey had suspected for some time that Nonna had arranged for her and Vito to go out with Daisy and Dion, knowing it would push them into acknowledging their feelings for each other.

Nonna patted Lacey's arm as if she were a bright student. "Yes, the whole matchmaking service was a scheme to get the two of you together. Of course, it's grown beyond that." Lou Ann and Miss Minnie had become Nonna's first lieutenants, matching up the singles of Rescue River.

"I'm just wondering when you three ladies will do some matchmaking on each other," Vito said. He didn't sound particularly surprised about Nonna's interference, either.

"Oh, no!" Nonna looked shocked. "We're having far too much fun to weigh ourselves down with cranky old men."

That made Lacey burst out laughing. "You're incorrigible."

"Well, and it didn't begin with the match-making service, either."

"What else?" Vito put on a mock-serious tone. "Tell us everything."

"I…well, I may have arranged for Lacey to take care of me, and my home to be unavailable, when I found out you were coming home, dear." She looked up through her glasses at Vito, her face tender. "You're going to be a wonderful husband, but I was afraid you'd be my age before you figured it out. When I ended up on Lacey's floor at the hospital, and heard about her history, and saw how lovely she'd grown up to be…well, I may have done a little scheming."

"Nonna D'Angelo!" Indignation warred with laughter in Lacey's heart. Laughter won on this glorious day.

"I have a way to make it up to you," Nonna said hastily. "You both know I came into a small inheritance when my cousin Paolo died last year."

Vito nodded, and Lacey just looked at Nonna, wondering where this was going. What would Nonna think of next?

"I've been trying to decide what use to make of it. What can I do, at my age? I have a few plans, but the first one is I want to give you this." She reached into her handbag and pulled out a small, gift wrapped box. She handed it to Lacey. "Open it."

The box was featherlight, and inside, there was nothing but paper. "I think you forgot to put the gift in—"

"Nonna!" Vito had pulled out the papers and was scanning them. "You can't do this!"

"I can, and I've already done it. You're booked for a week at a villa in Tuscany, and then a week in Rome and Venice. You leave tomorrow." She crossed her arms and smiled with satisfaction.

"But...our reservations in South Carolina..."

"Canceled. That was the interfering part." Nonna looked only slightly abashed. "You'll still get a wonderful honeymoon. It's just the destination that'll be different."

Lacey stared at Nonna and then at Vito. "Italy?" she asked faintly. "I've never been out of the country."

"And that's why your brother had to check into whether you had a passport. You do. Some trip to Canada that didn't material-ize?" Nonna waved her hand as if the de-tails didn't matter.

Lacey looked at Vito. "Italy."

"Together." A smile spread across his face. "I've never been, either."

"And that's why you need two weeks," Nonna said firmly. "Everything's all ar-ranged. The guesthouse, Charlie, reserva-tions in *Italia*."

Lacey looked up to see Buck, Charlie, Susan and Sam all crowded together, look-ing at them, coming over to congratulate them on their changed honeymoon schedule and destination. It looked like everyone had been in on the surprise. Even Charlie knew that he and Wolfie would get to spend a little longer at the dog rescue farm with Xavier.

A regular clinking and ringing sound came, the traditional instruction to kiss. Vito pulled Lacey into his arms and kissed her tenderly, then held her against his chest.

"Is this what it's going to be like to be married to you?" he rumbled into her ear. "Surprises and adventures?"

"Enough to keep you on your toes." She laughed up at him as he pulled her closer, and then looked beyond, to the clear blue sky. Vito was amazing, and life with him and Charlie was going to be an adventure.

But she knew deep inside that none of this was a surprise to her heavenly father, who'd orchestrated all of it and would guide them through the rest of their days.

* * * * *

Dear Reader,

Thank you for coming with me on another visit to Rescue River! Lacey has been a part of the Rescue River community from the beginning. Most recently, she was part of Buck and Gina's story, when she reluctantly provided shelter to the struggling single mom. Once everyone else found happiness, it was only fair that Lacey should find love, too…and Vito, the romantic Italian, seemed like just the right man to bring out Lacey's tender side.

Both Vito and Lacey carry scars and baggage from the past. Don't we all? Fortunately, our heavenly father forgives our mistakes and leads us to be new creations in Christ. He can even soften a heart of stone.

Visit my website, *www.leetobinmcclain.com*,

and sign up for my newsletter to keep track of all the news from Rescue River.

Wishing you a happy summer filled with many books!

Lee